BLOOD AND GOLD

When retired US Marshal Tom Stafford sets out for a new life, the past and future collide. A night stop in the town of Stratton brings love in the form of feisty Ella Farrell — as well as simmering tension and murder. But when Stafford gets wind that the man who ordered the deaths of his wife and child is close, he faces the prospect of confronting a lawless thug. And so he swears an oath: he'll take up his law badge again and eliminate his demons . . .

Books by Clay Starmer
in the Linford Western Library:

THE HIRED ACE
HELL AND THE HIGH S
ACE OF BONES

CLAY STARMER

◆

BLOOD AND GOLD

Complete and Unabridged

LINFORD
Leicester

First published in Great Britain in 2012 by
Robert Hale Limited
London

First Linford Edition
published 2014
by arrangement with
Robert Hale Limited
London

A catalogue record for this book is available
from the British Library.

ISBN 978–1–4448–2179–6

Published by
F. A. Thorpe (Publishing)
Anstey, Leicestershire

Set by Words & Graphics Ltd.
Anstey, Leicestershire
Printed and bound in Great Britain by
T. J. International Ltd., Padstow, Cornwall

This book is printed on acid-free paper

1

He'd arrived with dusk's first shadows — a stranger pushing through the batwings of the Rolling Cloud saloon. In time, with a shot of whiskey to hand, he'd adopted that downcast pose — slouched at the counter with his head lowered. He seemed, to those who ventured a view, both trail-worn and broken. His clothes bore days of dust. His face looked pinched by strain. Lastly, his eyes, if truly they were the windows on the soul, possessed the dull, sunken suggestion of unspeakable hurt.

As time ticked past — the saloon's clientele swelling and the atmosphere growing raucous — the stranger's melancholic posture set him starkly apart. It also riled the Cloud's balding proprietor, Frederick Smith.

This day, Smith's vexation brought

profanities to mind. That stranger at his bar — nothing but a saddle-bum — took up space and supped too slowly. His depressed attitude sullied the mood. More important, he wasn't the person Smith waited for.

Smith shook his head and mused angrily on his seemingly endless vigil for a certain man. His name Smith didn't know. He wasn't sure what he looked like. He possessed vital attributes though. He'd got ice for blood and no compunction over committing any act for the right price.

Yet still he didn't show. Instead, inebriates and no-goods cluttered the place. Quelling his ire, Smith moved away to tender more liquor. He'd leave that dead-beat stranger alone, mind. Any man — no matter what were his predilections — who bore a gun and stood so sombrely absorbed needed a wide berth. Whoever the drifter was, Smith assessed, he fled some dark and difficult past.

Or a tragic one?

Right then, exhausted and all too sober, Tom Stafford endured his shattering anguish. Lorna and Lizzie were gone. They'd died . . . no, someone had murdered them. Yet, whether God had taken them or a man with a gun, the result was the same: an aching space. After, it was the appalling reality of a solitary life. How could he go on?

Ride on to nowhere! He'd set west with a wad of dollars and his memories to sustain him. Sometimes — as now — he conjured images of his lost loves. Their faces filled his mind and he anchored them there. He wouldn't let them go . . . not again!

However, the images dissipated like wind-blown mist.

A touch to his arm was enough to drag Tom out of his cocoon of brooding and he spun round quickly, an angry curse shaping at his lips. He didn't utter it. Instead, he considered the middle-ager with the long beard and baleful eyes who now stood beside him.

'Mister,' that man said blandly,

'Things can't be *so* bad?'

Tom fought his fury.

'What the hell do you know?' He spat at the boards before locking the long-beard with a venomous glare. 'I don't recall sending you an invite.'

The bearded man's countenance clouded. Then, shrugging, he jabbed a finger at two others seated at a nearby table.

'We're pan men,' he said, unfazed. 'We're set to Cheyenne Heights.' He shrugged. 'Our wagon-wheel busted. We camped out until some soldier boys set by. We're late to this site.'

Tom's eyes blazed but he swallowed down his rage. Then he dropped a hand to his pocket and hauled out some coins.

'Here,' he barked, slamming the money on the counter. 'Drown your goddamn sorrows.'

The man's eyes widened. 'Mister, we've got dollars enough.' He shook his head. 'I set here to get *you* a drink.'

Tom's isolation and anger melted like

spring snow. Swamped with regret, he mused despondently on what he'd become: a nomadic, dishevelled husk of the man he'd once been. Cursing at his own spoken bile, Tom resolved to make quick amends.

'Look,' he said, 'my apologies. Things have been tough.' He proffered a forced smile. 'I'd be obliged for a whiskey.'

Soon, Tom was seated at the miners' table with a fresh measure of redeye to hand. For weeks now he'd communicated but sparingly with anyone. He'd remedy that: a spell in amiable company might prove a restorative boost.

In the minutes that followed the miners told all.

'We've panned north to south for years,' drawled one. 'This time, so help us, we'll strike rich and then we retire.' He shrugged. 'It's not the best life.'

Tom sipped at the redeye and pondered about that. He'd heard tales of the mining camps — sprawling shanties of canvas and plank inhabited by rough and desperate men. Gold brought out the worst aspects of the human condition and violence inevitably followed.

'You've done all right,' he observed drily. 'You're alive and you've got greenbacks to spend.'

'We've avoided trouble,' the miner intoned, 'up 'til now. Fact is, we're older and I'd rather trust to a gun.' He eyed Tom intently. 'If others know you've got a quick draw beside you they'll leave you be.'

Tom's eyes narrowed. 'What the — '

'We've watched you,' the miner replied, topping Tom's glass. 'You keep your own counsel, which is good.' His intense look mellowed to one of hope. 'That skull inlaid on your Colt butt suggests you're useful with a gun.'

Tom sighed. 'OK, you've done your homework.' He underscored his comprehension with a curt nod. 'So you're after protection?'

The miner shrugged. 'If we find nuggets we aim to keep them.' He nodded then. 'We'll pay well for your services.'

Tom frowned. He'd drifted since leaving Cedarville, his money constantly being depleted. Although he still had funds enough, a chance to replenish what he'd spent he couldn't ignore. More vital, in a way, was that occupying his time might distract him from his sombre introspection.

'Listen,' he drawled wearily, 'I'll consider the offer.' He drained his glass and set it aside. 'I've ridden some miles and I need rest. Set here at noon tomorrow and I'll . . . '

His words stilled as the batwings crashed. Swinging his gaze, Tom considered the man who'd just booted through the doors. A big brute for sure — six foot and more of denim-clad muscle — the entrant's voluble grunt preceded giant strides towards the counter. He'd made about half that distance when the batwings clattered again.

The woman who now showed seemed

7

driven by rage. Her auburn hair flailed
as she ran, her eyes — a hue of stirred
jade — anchored their gaze to the bruis-
er's back. She got to him fast, clawing
fingernails to his neck.

As she wounded him, she yelled
words thick with venom.

'You scum, Duggan, you'll pay what's
owed!'

Duggan, howling as her nails drew
blood, spun and shrugged her off. With
her balance thrown, she fought to stay
on her feet whilst the big man laughed.

She moved forward as if to attack
again, but then, her face crumpling, she
sank to her knees. When her head
slumped, her body rocked with sup-
pressed sobs.

Duggan snorted and completed his
route to the bar. 'Anyone crosses me,'
he roared, slamming a fist on the
redwood counter, 'they'll get beat like
the livery bitch.' His face contorted to a
snarl. 'Smith, I want redeye now!'

The saloon-owner, his features pas-
sive, reached for a bottle and dispensed

a shot. This whiskey, when Duggan had it to hand, he sniffed at like a connoisseur. At last, nodding his approval, the big man inched the glass to his lips.

It didn't get there.

Something smacked into Duggan's side and drove the drink from his grasp. With the redeye spilled, Duggan spun with hell in his eyes.

'Jeez I'll — '

Tom, who'd crossed the saloon's boards at a sprint, fixed Duggan with a steady gaze.

'What you'll do,' he cut in, 'is help the lady up.'

Duggan's jaw muscles tightened and he considered Tom with an icy stare. 'That bitch,' he spat, 'is of no account.' He jabbed a bulbous thumb at Tom's chest. 'You don't stick in this town's business, drifter!'

Tom's look suggested that he would brook no dissension. 'Listen, lughead,' he said calmly. 'Help the lady up and get on your own knees. Then you'll beg forgiveness.'

Duggan snorted a laugh.

'You're something else. Now, I'll beat you dead for it.'

He lurched with speed, his huge hands grasping Tom's coat and dragging him forward. Now, Duggan's face pressed against his own, Tom felt nauseated by the other's foul-scented breath.

He achieved rapid relief. He dragged out his Colt and dispatched a slug that ripped into Duggan's right foot.

With the roar of Tom's gun bellowing in his ears the big man paled. His face contorted then, his eyes widening as the pain bit. He loosed his hold and collapsed on to his back on the sawdust-strewn floor. Sprawled there, with his wounded limb held aloft, he groaned loudly.

Quickly, though, another sound caught Tom's attention.

A voice — certain and pressing — cut in above Duggan's pain-racked moaning.

'Set down that pistol, mister, or I'll spread brains.'

Tom, turning slowly, peered down the muzzle of a rifle. The man wielding the weapon, his creased skin suggestive of age, bore a sheriff's badge on his vest.

Tom locked the lawman's gaze with an assured stare. 'This shooting's justified. The big oaf attacked me first.'

The lawman's eyes sparked with distrust. He jabbed out with that Winchester he held. 'It's damn lucky I was passing. Now, toss aside that Colt. I won't ask again.'

Tom bristled, a string of profane invective at his lips, but he didn't get the chance to utter it.

The woman was on her feet again. She cast a brief desirous glance towards Tom, then set her attention to the lawman. 'No, Alf Canning,' she yelled. 'Leave him be.'

'But Ella,' growled the sheriff, 'he shot Duggan in the son-of-a-bitch foot.'

'It's been due,' she snapped. 'Duggan wouldn't pay his fees and when I sought to get the money he beat on me.

The drifter tried to help.' She sighed. 'Duggan owes me dollars.'

When Duggan had gone, helped out of the saloon lighter by four coins, Sheriff Canning fixed Tom with a scything glare.

'I ought to run you in for causing injury. I won't, though.' He shook his head. 'I don't deny Fleet Duggan had it coming, but any more trouble and I'll be on you like molasses.'

The sheriff spun round and departed with a curse, leaving Tom to bed his gun and take stock of what had happened. He sighed, then stepped across to the woman.

'Why, ma'am, I — '

She leapt at him like a pained wildcat. Fighting off the blows, Tom finally subdued them by enveloping her in a hug.

'Hands off, you stinking cur,' she screeched. 'You stinking no-good man. Let me be, pig!'

'I will, missy,' bellowed Tom, bemused. 'I don't get it. I deal with that thug

Duggan and you're clawing at me.'

Her assault subsided, her body sagged and her head pressed to his chest.

'Pig,' she said breathlessly. 'Men can't be trusted.'

Tom, shocked by the attraction he felt, released his hold and she stepped away. A moment later, eying him intently she delivered some tremulous words.

'You're riding through?'

Tom shrugged. 'I aim to get under a roof for the night.'

She nodded. 'You can stick your carcass in our hayloft, on account of helping. We got us the livery. It'll reek of horses but it'll do.' She did her best for a smile before she pointed at the batwings. 'Hurry it up and you can have food too.'

Tom turned to look at the miners. 'Fellers, I just don't — '

'Good night,' returned one, doffing his hat. 'We hope to see you tomorrow. You're surely the man we need.'

Behind the counter, Fred Smith dried his hands with a towel and mused on the same idea. He quickly dismissed it. Sure, the drifter who'd dealt with Duggan, far from being a loser, had shown himself mightily impressive. Trouble was, he'd garnered the attention of Sheriff Canning and gone off with Ella from the livery. That wouldn't do at all.

Smith turned and grabbed for a bottle. Or would it?

2

In the dilapidated drinking-shack of some no-account town, Lucas Cole and Caleb Stark quaffed redeye. In time, with half the bottle consumed, Stark voiced his simmering intentions.

'Next stop's Stratton,' he growled. 'After that we get to those Cheyenne Heights.'

Lucas, with both feet rested up on a chair, pondered about gold. Stark had been convinced from the first, Lucas anything but. Gold fever struck often in these newly opened lands; it usually produced nothing but violence and disappointment.

'You reckon it's true?' Lucas intoned. 'That man what said it was right drunk. It might be lies.'

Stark shrugged. 'I reckon so. I heard of a find in Nebraska where nuggets just lay up on the slopes.'

Lucas frowned with doubt. Stark's half-cocked ideas and trigger-happy nature always led to trouble. Yet, Lucas mused, he always acceded to Stark's reckless schemes in the end.

'Yeah, Cal,' he muttered. 'I suppose — ' He stopped short, his feet went to ground fast and he clapped his hand on the butt of his Colt .41. Stark, his own Peacemaker drawn, had caution in his eyes.

They both bristled and listened. That noise, drifting in through the saloon's half-open door, always set wanted men on edge. When it quieted, the drum of hoofbeats petering out to the snort of spent horses, Stark shook his head and slid the Peacemaker into his lap.

Time slowed then — tension-layered moments through which Stark and Lucas considered their crimes. Right now, out there on that dustbowl road, men seeking bounty might be girding their nerves.

Lucas broke first. 'Hell, Cal,' he

16

hissed, 'what if — '

His words choked out as the door whined. When that creaking stilled, two shadows were spread across the shack's rotting boards.

Lucas, sweat beading his brow, twitched fingers over his gun. Stark, though, dispelled his tension with a deep sigh. This pair at the door, he sensed, presented no threat. When they moved in, Stark bedded his gun. These were not the law or those dollar-hunting dogs at the peripheries of it. Quite who they were only liquor-fuelled talk would reveal.

It wouldn't take long. The incomers, their steps made tuneful by spurs, crossed the saloon before grunting into chairs. Whilst one produced makings and built a smoke, the other slid off his Stetson and fixed Stark with a searching glare.

'How far,' he gasped, his words husked by thirst, 'is Cheyenne Heights?'

Stark smirked. 'We're not sure.' He jabbed a thumb at the bottle. 'You'll drink? It seems we're set to the same spot.'

The other nodded. 'I'm O'Malley. My partner here is Lee Fielding.' He shrugged. 'You don't look like pan men.'

Stark shrugged. 'Nor do you.'

Now O'Malley grinned. 'OK, mister.' He gestured a hand at the barkeep. 'Bring more redeye and then get lost.'

Soon, all four of them were seated about the same table. With the whiskey biting, they shared their tales.

Stark and Cole, Arkansas men, were habitual robbers. Stark's propensity for slaughter, though, complicated matters. Wanted by that state and several others, they'd set their aim further west until Stark had been beguiled by that mention of gold.

O'Malley and Fielding had ridden a different course. Former soldiers drummed out for drunkenness, they'd slipped to the wrong side of the law. They, too, beguiled with the chatter about wealth at Cheyenne Heights, were heading there with profit in mind.

When talk ended, O'Malley slapped his discharge paper on the table. 'There, that'll prove the truth.'

Stark nodded and reached into his jacket. He pulled out a sheet of crumpled paper and worked it open.

O'Malley read it and frowned. 'That's you, sure enough.' He shook his head. 'So you're a hunted man, eh? Well, tell me this: how'd you get hold of your own Wanted poster?'

'Some place in Arkansas,' drawled Stark. 'Say, O'Malley, what do heinous villain mean?'

O'Malley topped up his glass and smirked. 'It means you're evil, Stark. That might be useful where we're going!'

* * *

Tom slid into a seat at the kitchen table and watched whilst Ella ladled stew on to a plate.

'You're lucky,' she said sternly as she

19

dished the food. 'Or I'd have kicked your useless man-hide out of town.'

Tom grinned. Her feisty persona enlivened a middle-aged woman of handsome looks. That red hair glowed; those alluring green-hued eyes settled on him just too often.

He dismissed his stirred feelings as she set the over-filled plate on the table before him.

'Say,' he muttered between mouthfuls of the delicious meal. 'You sure don't like men.'

'Hell I don't.' She sank into a chair. 'This town's full of bums, drifters and pan dogs. They'd rob you soon as spit.' She sighed. 'Alf Canning — he can't deal with it.'

Tom nodded and set back to his meal. Afterwards, Ella having stared at him intently until he'd cleared the plate, Tom laid the fork aside and shook his head.

'So times are tough in Stratton, then?'

Ella frowned. 'It's not just miners like

Fleet Duggan,' she said with passion. 'Others set in: men that just make you shiver. You know what I mean by that?'

Tom didn't answer. Instead, he took makings out of a pocket and built a cigarette. He fixed her then with a curious look.

'I'm Tom Stafford, Mrs . . . ?'

'Farrell,' she said. 'I live here with my pa.' Her countenance clouded. 'And you, Mr Stafford . . . why are you here?'

Tom paused, unsure. He hadn't discussed it with a living soul. Yet, right here, right now, with this perfect stranger, he got an urge to discuss it all. After he'd spoken she wore a look of shock.

'Dear Lord, your wife and child — I mean, how?'

'I was away at the time. Lizzie wanted to get me a welcome-home gift. The man who killed them was some psychopath who'd been released from Cedarville's jail.'

Her face paled. 'Good God! How did you . . . ?' Her words trailed off and she expressed a look of utter horror.

'I buried my wife and child,' said Tom drily, 'and I set back to work. I couldn't stay there, though. Eventually, a few months back, I resigned. I sold our house and here I am.'

'Headed through,' she gasped. 'And after all that's happened you're still tackling thugs, but without the badge?'

Tom frowned. 'I reckon that's part of me that will never change.' He looked at her, curious. 'Say, Ella, if I hadn't stuck in, would any of the locals have helped you out? Hell, Duggan's a big brute, right enough!'

'I don't need any man's . . . ' She stilled her outburst, her face colouring. She shrugged. 'Folk mind their own affairs, or those that choose to stay in town do. Most people leave.'

'I don't get it,' muttered Tom. 'The miners bring trade?'

'It's no trade that we want,' she said sourly. 'They get drunk, smash up places and then ride off to the hills. Those that stable their horses are like

Fleet Duggan. You do the work and they don't want to pay. Then more come and do the same.'

'Yet you and your pa have stayed?'

She looked embarrassed. 'Our business and home are in hock to a bank. Unless things change, we'll lose it all. There's no hope in hell we'll sell the livery, so we're stuck.'

Tom nodded. 'I'm sorry.' He climbed wearily to his feet. 'That meal was grand. Thanks. I'd reckon to get some sleep now.'

An old man suddenly appeared in the kitchen doorway and Ella said, 'This is my father.' Her face set determined then. 'Pa,' she barked, 'this man's horse we'll stable as a guest. He'll sleep in our spare room.'

The old man looked aghast. 'But we can't — '

'Hush, Pa,' she snapped. 'I know what I'm doing.' She fixed Tom with a non-negotiable stare. 'Fetch your horse. I'll get your bedroom ready.'

When Tom hesitated, she pushed him

towards the door.

The old man frowned. 'She don't do arguing with, no matter how big they are.'

'So I've seen,' said Tom. He pinned Ella with a confirming stare. 'So I'll set back here?'

She gulped and eventually turned away. Before she did though, their eyes locked long enough to make his blood surge.

3

They reached Stratton as the clocks inched into midnight. They hitched their horses at the back of town and set off to Main Street on foot. They got there just in time — rain was descending fast as they arrived. Soon, with thunder crashing over the settlement, they strode a boardwalk to the Rolling Cloud saloon.

'I've got to say,' exclaimed O'Malley as they viewed a line of wagons trundling along the thoroughfare, which had rapidly become sodden, 'it looks like this gold strike's bigger than we thought.'

Inside the Rolling Cloud, which was sparsely populated and deathly quiet, they saw a muscular man with his bandaged foot propped up on a chair. The man's eyes, as they neared, were as red as blood.

He struggled to focus but gave a strained grin.

'Howdy.' He pointed jerkily at Stark. 'Your fayshe is all scarred.' He laughed inanely. 'I got me a scar as well!'

O'Malley and Fielding slouched against the bar and ordered beer. Stark and Lucas pulled chairs up to a table and dropped into them with grunts of weariness.

'Whiskey,' called out Stark. 'Tender, bring it over.'

Fred Smith, snorting with contempt, reached for a bottle and slammed it on the counter top. He glared intently at Lucas. 'Tell your partner I don't serve at table.'

Lucas, weary and frowning, grunted to his feet and collected the whiskey. When he got back to the table he passed the redeye to Stark before retaking his seat with an audible curse.

Stark, taking a sizeable swig, emitted a chuckle.

'You can't get anything easy any more.' He swung in his seat and set a considered look at the only other customers — three bearded men. 'Say,' he drawled, 'you're set to the heights?'

One of the miners, redeye fuelling his nerve, scowled back.

'That's our goddamn business.'

Stark's narrowed eyes became slits of sinister intent. When he spoke, he drilled his words through gritted teeth.

'What the hell did you say?'

Lucas, worry turning his guts, inched up in his seat. 'Jeez, Cal,' he growled. 'Let's just leave it, eh?'

Stark wasn't listening. He rose to his feet and spat at the boards. Jabbing a hand, Stark growled, 'This man's got the guts to say stuff so he'll answer for it.'

The miner sobered fast. He sat upright, his face paled.

'I didn't mean offence,' he spluttered. Right then, in the confines of the late-hour saloon, Stark's facial scar and dark, harsh eyes instilled gut-turning fear.

'Yeah,' gasped one of the other

long-beards. 'Forget it. We got it wrong.'

A loud howl made Stark turn. He watched, momentarily distracted, as the man with the bandaged foot crashed off his chair to land on the boards in a cloud of smacked-up sawdust.

Stark's gaze swung, settling piercingly on the barkeep. Smith, disturbed and absorbed in equal measure, weighed it in his mind but then decided to see how matters resolved. Then, shrugging, the saloon-owner disappeared quickly through a door at the rear of the bar.

At the counter, O'Malley and Fielding felt rising disquiet. Although neither spoke, their swapped glances said it all. They put flagons aside and settled hands to their guns.

Time inched by, the Rolling Cloud sparking with tension. In that silent hiatus, the three miners willed themselves away. Suddenly, though, it all changed.

Stark laughed. 'Boys, I'm only messing.'

The relief was palpable. The trio of

miners — thankfulness etched on their faces — exchanged smiles.

'OK,' one gasped. 'We'll set to our wagon and head out.'

Stark frowned. 'A wagon, eh? You've got supplies enough?'

The man looked confused. He shrugged before muttering nervously, 'Err . . . yeah, we've got stock to last.'

Stark shook his head. 'Where's your team lashed?'

The miners' words came layered with suspicion. 'They're under awnings at the edge of town.' The pan man's eyes flashed with doubt. 'Grove Street. You're after buying something?'

'No,' intoned Stark. 'I only buy liquor and dames.'

Slowly then, each movement made with caution, the three miners got to their feet and set toward the batwings. They'd almost achieved the swing doors when Stark's call made them halt.

'And where are you bastards going?'

The pan men turned, their drained

faces pinched with fear.

'We'll leave,' said one softly, 'and let you alone.'

'Yeah,' spat Stark, dragging up his Colt, 'Leave you will!'

Stark's Colt roared. For the next hellish moments, through a riot of sheet flame and smoke, slugs spat from the outlaw's gun and ripped across the room. A bullet tore into one man's throat — dropping him like a rock to lie blood-drenched and dying on the Rolling Cloud's sawdust-coated timbers. More lead ripped into another's head, slamming into that man with sickening force. He'd perished before he hit the ground, his crumpled cadaver testament to that. When the third miner's life ended, blasted in the back as he tried to escape, his body plunged forward to lie across a table.

Now, the noise and gunsmoke dissipating, Stark slid the Colt into its holster and shrugged. 'That's finished then.'

Lucas lurched to his feet. 'Jeez, Cal,' he spat. 'What the hell have you done?'

'Yeah,' drawled another voice. 'What *have* you done?'

Stark's jerked gaze lit upon the barkeep back at the counter.

'That shooting,' drawled Smith, 'will bring folk here fast. Unless you'd welcome a rawhide end I'd suggest you get out.'

Stark's look clouded. He levelled his gun and his finger twitched at the trigger, but something in that saloon-man's forceful eyes bade Stark not to shoot. He lowered the Colt and anchored the barkeep with a withering glare.

'You best be playing this straight or, God's teeth, I'll — '

'Mister,' Smith spat, 'you've butchered three unarmed men in my saloon. That makes you plumb crazy in my book, but I'm giving you a way out.' He shook his head. 'Are you taking escape or will you be here arguing when the law steps in?'

Stark nodded at the others. Quickly then, following Smith's pointed direction, they stepped behind the counter. They halted briefly, Smith applying a blocking arm to Stark's chest.

'Your gun,' the saloon owner snapped, 'It's needed.'

Stark's lips shaped to a curse but he didn't utter it. Instead, fighting his seething suspicion, he passed the Colt over.

Smith moved fast. He strode to the unconscious Duggan and pressed Stark's .45 into the man's limp hand. Deftly, he closed Duggan's fingers about the butt before dragging Fleet's own Schofield from its holster.

'You got to lie low,' Smith growled as he proffered Duggan's weapon. He produced a key from a pocket. 'There's a rundown farm south of town. I'll meet you there sometime tomorrow.'

Stark, bedding the Schofield, spat. 'If this is a trick?'

'It's not,' growled Smith, jabbing a hand at the doorway to the rear of the saloon. 'I swear. Now, get going.'

At that, they fled.

* * *

Tom sat up with a start. He gasped against an aching dryness at his throat, then he pressed his head back against the wall. He held there, willing his pounding heart to still. When it did, he battled weariness and a gut-turning disquiet over what had woken him. Soon, his eyes adjusting to the dark, he listened to the drumming intensity of the rain. It lashed the livery — a deluge smacking against the window and hammering down on to the roof.

It was that, Tom mused now, that had stirred him from his slumber. He sighed and began to drop his head back to the pillow. A new sound made him pause, though — an insistent rapping on the door.

When the knocking sound ceased, a voice sounded. It was Ella. 'Tom Stafford, are you awake?'

Puzzled, Tom got out of bed and opened the door.

Ella, clad in a nightgown and brandishing a lamp, glanced up the corridor before pinning Tom with a potent stare.

'You hear that?' she hissed.

'It's a storm,' said Tom. 'You're a mite over the age to be frightened of such.'

Ella's fatigued features showed fury then. Her eyes widened and sparked with anger whilst her lips shaped to a curse.

'Gunshots,' she snapped. 'I counted three at least. It came from somewhere along Main Street.' Her body trembled in a shudder that made the lamp flame jump. 'We get slugs loosed in town all the time now,' she blurted, 'but never this late.'

Tom shook his head. 'Thunder . . . I slept through it.'

'It weren't thunder,' she barked. 'It's guns sure enough.'

'Your pa,' said Tom, impatience in his

words. 'Don't he — '

She pushed past him into the room and those jade eyes now flickered with fear. Setting the lamp on a table, she stifled a sob. When she spoke, her words shook.

'Pa's asleep. Nothing wakes him. I really am scared.' She scanned his face before dropping her gaze.

'I'll be,' said Tom. 'All your feisty fire's clean out.'

Her gaze lifted and she drilled him with a bitter glare.

'Blast you,' she spat. 'It'd be a fool that didn't scare at guns.' Her face crumpled. 'Oh, go to hell, why'd I bother?'

She set towards the door, but Tom threw out a hand and clutched her gently at the wrist.

She didn't struggle, simply muttered, 'The shooting?'

'Please,' he muttered, 'stay awhile.'

'Mr Stafford,' she said shakily, 'I just don't — '

'Stay or go,' he growled. 'I don't

know what else to say.' He sat down on the edge of the bed.

She dropped down beside him. 'I hate men,' she hissed.

'No, ma'am?' said Tom. 'I reckon not.'

She leant closer and their lips met in a lingering kiss.

Later, when an image of his late wife began to evolve in his mind, he quelled it before it had fully formed. An ache of longing overtook all other considerations. An hour after, lying together, she whispered in his ear, 'You'll stay in Stratton?'

He didn't answer. They kissed again and night clothed their passion.

*   *   *

Fred Smith set the shot of whiskey on the counter top and watched with a scowl as Stratton's sheriff stepped forward.

Canning lifted the glass, put it to his lips and drained the redeye in one swallow. With his guts burning, the sheriff shifted his gaze to view again the blood-spattered corpses.

'Jeez,' Canning gasped. 'I can't believe it.'

Smith stepped out from the bar and approached the comatose Fleet Duggan. He prodded the big man's side with his boot. 'Goddamn son-of-a-bitch killer.'

Canning set the glass aside and moved across. He cursed as he walked. Fate, that fickle master, meant he'd missed the killings by minutes. He'd locked up the jail, satisfied that the rain had quieted the town for the night and set along the boardwalk for his home. He'd just turned into an alley when those gun blasts raged out.

Right now, at the scene of the slaughter, he bent down and lifted the Colt Peacemaker from the unconscious Fleet's grip. The muzzle felt warm to the touch. Canning checked the chamber. Two bullets remained.

'He never loaded six,' growled Smith. 'Three slugs spent. It's one for each of them sorry dogs lying dead there.'

The sheriff nodded and cursed at himself. He'd known Duggan for months — that towering, drunkard pan man had been causing nuisance enough — but never once had Canning noted the gun that Duggan wore at his hip. Jeez, Canning seethed in his mind, *I'm losing it*.

He challenged the Rolling Cloud's owner with an intense look. 'If what you say is right it seems cut and dry, I reckon.'

Fury sparked in Smith's eyes. 'Are you saying I'm lying, Canning? It was just Fleet and those three and I heard shouts. Then gun blasts sounded.' Smith shrugged. 'Well, you see it all!'

Canning frowned. 'Duggan were fainted out like that?'

'God's teeth, Fleet was drunk to the gills and yelling fit to burst. I heard Fleet raving about killing on account of being shot in the foot.' Smith fixed the sheriff with an accusing glare. 'It's not for me to question, but folk in town might ask why that business earlier weren't dealt with?'

'Now hold it,' snapped Canning. 'I didn't have an option. Fleet beat up on Ella and he got what he deserved. Hell, a slug in the foot was long overdue for the goddamn animal.'

'Sheriff,' returned Smith mockingly. 'I'm not accusing you. Stay a bit.' The saloon-owner retook his place behind the counter and topped up the lawman's glass. 'Let it — '

A clatter of the batwings swamped his words. The men who entered — half a dozen locals led by a short middle-ager with horn-rimmed spectacles — came to an abrupt stop. They all regarded the bodies with looks of despair.

'Oh, no,' howled the bespectacled one. 'What in hell?'

Canning shook his head. 'The killer's there, Mayor Gill. The matter's done with, save for a judge and the hanging.'

The rest of the men dragged Fleet up on to his feet.

'What'll we do?' Stratton's mayor intoned dejectedly.

'Send for the judge,' said Canning briskly. 'Then we'll discuss a deputy.' He swung his gaze to the locals holding on to Fleet. 'I'd be obliged if you men would lodge Duggan in the jail.'

When Fleet had been dragged out Gill sank into a chair with a groan. 'This is all we need,' he muttered, dabbing at his forehead with a handkerchief. 'There're few enough folk to pay for officials.' He shook his head. 'Still, I'll see what I can do.'

'It was only a matter of time,' said Canning drily. 'The Rolling Cloud's about the only place that's benefitted from this gold madness. It's full of drunks and thugs from noon till night.'

Gill got to his feet and set towards the batwings. He halted, then spun round and shook his head.

'Don't leave, Alf. I'll do what I can about an assistant.'

Fred Smith scoffed. 'Stay it, Mayor. Let the man hang up his badge. It's well known that he can't keep order.'

The sheriff's look darkened. 'Go to hell, Smith. We all know what your gripe is.'

'Stay it,' bellowed Gill. 'That stuff between you two is done with. Right now we got a triple murder to deal with.'

When Gill had gone Canning fixed Smith with a scathing glare.

'I'll get Albert to shift those corpses.'

Smith shrugged. 'It's late, Sheriff. Leave it 'til the morning.' The saloon-owner chuckled. 'I mean, Jeez . . . it's not as if they'll be drinking my stock while I sleep.'

The sheriff of Stratton felt his guts lurch and he plunged into the rain-lashed street.

4

'Good morning, Mr Stafford.' Ella proffered a broad grin. 'I trust your overnight stay was a satisfactory one?'

Tom dropped into a chair and nodded. He'd awoken to streaming light, the curtains open and Ella gone from his side. Getting up, he'd noticed the tin tub with its steaming fill of water. He soaked for an hour, every worry and ache erased in that hot fluid. Afterwards he'd dried himself with a towel she'd left on the dresser, got into his clothes and headed downstairs.

Right now, he considered her with both lust and worry.

'Ella,' he muttered, 'I just wanted . . .'

She stepped across and answered with a lingering kiss. 'Please stay awhile, Tom. No need to leave, surely?'

He shrugged. 'I'll eat and then I've got to speak to some men. They offered work but I'll tell them I've changed my mind.'

Half an hour more and he left the house. Pausing briefly in the street outside, he glanced through the livery doors. Inside, Ella's father jabbed at the forge coals with a poker. He noticed Tom and gave a friendly enough nod.

'I'm told,' Stanley drawled, 'you're not going just yet?'

Tom shrugged. 'Ella says — '

'She says a lot,' cut in the liveryman. 'She says there was a storm last night but I didn't hear a thing.' He chuckled and shook his head. 'Ride a horse through my bedroom and I wouldn't know about it.'

Tom grinned and moved on. Soon, as he progressed along a boardwalk he saw a sign stating the settlement's resident population to be 762. It was more likely, Tom mused, with all the mining activity, that the number of people currently in the town would significantly exceed that.

A local man soon confirmed it.

'All rough sorts stop here.' The man shook his head. 'Trouble is, decent families leave and those that replace them you wouldn't trust an inch.' He shrugged. 'Talking of trouble — that shooting last night was a bad business!'

Tom felt a stab of disquiet. Ella had been right about the gun sounds she'd heard above the rain's slamming deluge. He'd dismissed it as nothing more than frightened imaginings.

'A shooting, you say?' Tom pressed. 'What happened?'

The old man shrugged. 'I only know what I heard. It's said there's been killings in the Rolling Cloud saloon.'

Hiding his surprise, Tom pushed on. He left the boardwalk, taking a route up the centre of Main Street. Right now, just past 10 a.m., the thoroughfare bustled with movement — people criss-crossing the rutted earth strip whilst a line of wagons kept a sedate pace to the town's western edge.

Tom lost little time. He got to the steps outside the Rolling Cloud and ascended at a jog. Once at the batwings, he set a hand to the doors but pulled away as they opened for him. He held there then, watching in nauseated disbelief as men carried out the corpses of the three miners he'd talked to the day before. Shock numbed Tom's mind and he struggled to comprehend what he'd just seen. These deaths, though they lacked the same personal significance as losing his wife and child, still winded him by their suddenness.

When he'd beaten down his dismay Tom glanced about, to see the board-walk cleared and the sheriff leaving the saloon.

Canning stilled, his head lowering a moment before he anchored Tom with a seething glare.

'Three men butchered,' he growled. 'It's a shame.'

Tom's eyes sparked with anger.

'A shame you say? Jeez — those men have been murdered.' He gulped down a curse and spat at the planks. 'They'd offered me gun work. Hell, I was set to meet them at midday to discuss it.'

Canning's icy attitude changed. He pushed back the brim of his Stetson before pointing to the jailhouse across the street.

'Come on, let's talk.'

Before long, seated in the law office, Tom set aside a mug of coffee and began to build a cigarette. Soon, he blew out a perfect ring of grey, scented smoke and related the previous day's events.

'Dear God,' remarked Canning as Tom finished. 'They wanted protection but they didn't get it.'

'Now hang on,' snapped Tom, 'I hadn't agreed — '

'I'm not blaming you,' growled the sheriff, dragging out a drawer of his desk and producing a bottle of whiskey. He put out two glasses and dispensed the drink. 'Like you said — you'd set to meet them today to discuss it. What went on in that saloon can't be . . . ' he trailed off shaking his head. When he spoke again, he muttered words edged with concern. 'In a way you and I *might* get the blame for these killings.'

Tom's countenance clouded. 'I don't understand.'

The sheriff's stare was piercing. 'Fleet Duggan — that big oaf you blasted in the foot — he murdered those three men.'

Tom's guts lurched. 'Jeez, so the son of a bitch got back into the saloon.' He shook his head. 'I only tried to help Ella.'

'A shooting should've got you locked up,' said Canning blandly. 'I'll be cursed at for not slamming you in the cells.'

'It wouldn't have stopped the killings,' said Tom testily. 'If Duggan had been barred from the saloon those miners would be living still.'

Canning shrugged. 'True enough. Anyhow, Duggan's been on borrowed time.' He gestured to the rear of the jailhouse. 'He's sleeping off enough liquor. The whole block reeks of it.'

Tom went to rise but the sheriff's

words halted him.

'Tell me, Stafford — so you're in the gun game?'

Tom shrugged. 'I'd planned to protect three gold-miners. Right now, I need to look at other options.' He did get to his feet then, making quick strides across the jailhouse.

'I take it,' persisted Canning as Tom reached the door, 'that you stayed at Ella's place last night?'

Tom spun angrily. 'Don't you — '

'Stay it,' drawled Canning, unfazed. 'I'm not interested in what you and she do. I just thought I'd let you know . . . ' He fought to subdue a smirk. 'She was wed before. Warren his name was. He took up with the wife of Fred Smith — him what owns the Rolling Cloud. Neither Ella nor Smith knew a thing about it.'

A seismic shock jolted Tom. Indignation turned his guts but he couldn't reason why. Ella had a past — as did he — but he'd been honest and open. She'd said nothing.

'Yeah,' Canning pressed on. 'When that affair came out it caused a heck of a lot of trouble.' The sheriff swigged more whiskey. He pinned Tom with a searching look. 'Smith's son settled it.'

Tom's curiosity got the better of him. 'Goddamn it — how?'

Canning shrugged. 'Smith's boy blasted Ella's husband and his own mother when he found them . . . ' The sheriff sighed. 'Well, I don't need to draw you a picture, I'd reckon?'

Tom's eyes narrowed. 'Boy?'

Canning shook his head. 'He was old enough to swing.' The sheriff leant back in his chair. 'Listen, Stafford, I've told you as it is. This town's seen some murders in its time and now there's these latest to deal with.'

Tom, quelling his agitation, said, 'Some crazy, drunk miner shot three others. Your killer is locked up.'

'Yeah,' returned Canning, looking expectant now. 'You said about options. I need a deputy. The way you dealt with Duggan might make you useful. I need a person to back me up. I'll retire before long. How'd it sound: Sheriff of Stratton?'

Tom grimaced. 'I'm not your man.'

'Ella and her pa,' Canning went on, 'are struggling, I hear.' He waited for a response but when none came, he growled, 'Fair enough, Stafford. Pass on through. We'll still be here if or when you happen this way again. That gold bubble might have burst by then and Stratton will be back to dying slowly.'

Tom didn't answer. He went outside to the boardwalk and was bout to step away. He stayed, though, Canning's call making him ponder.

'They're good people in this town, Stafford. They'll give their last cent to pay for law. That means a lot, I'd say.' A pause followed before Canning cried, 'Does that mean anything to you, Tom Stafford?'

5

Stark gazed through a cracked window-pane at the vista beyond. Flat grassland stretched from the farmhouse yard, with its array of ramshackle timber buildings all the way to Stratton.

He turned and watched as Lucas prodded at the embers in the grate with a stick. Soon, flames writhed up and Lucas added fresh logs.

Stark sighed. A run-down farmstead, the barkeep had said. He hadn't been wrong. The barn and other sheds displayed the gaps of neglect but they'd provided sufficient shelter for the horses.

He moved across the room and slid into a seat, musing intently on the previous night's events. They'd got doubly lucky. As well as the assistance of the saloon-owner to flee the town, they'd located the miners' wagon, which Lucas had driven to the farm. From the buckboard of that vehicle they'd removed food stores and cooking gear. Four pristine bottles of whiskey had been an unexpected reward. It meant they'd all slept soundly, heated by a night fire, which Lucas was now resurrecting.

O'Malley and Fielding gathered up their bedrolls from the floor and slid into chairs around the kitchen table.

'Stark,' drawled O'Malley, building a smoke. 'Your Wanted poster's right enough: you're some unstable son of a bitch.'

Stark shrugged. 'You got a problem with killing?'

'Yeah,' O'Malley drawled. 'I do if it puts my neck in a noose. Jeez, you can't blast every cur who talks out of turn.'

Stark lunged for his gun.

'Quit riling me, Irish,' he snarled. 'I'll — '

'Bed that piece,' grunted O'Malley, unperturbed. He gave a shrug. 'What's done can't be changed. What I don't get is that beer-tender. Hell, you slay three people in his bar and he helps us get away. What in God's teeth is *that* about?'

'If it's a trap,' opined Fielding, taking a mug of coffee from Lucas, 'we'll be like fish in a barrel.'

Stark sheathed the pistol. 'That barkeep said he'd be here. If he doesn't — ' He stopped abruptly as a clatter sounded outside.

Fielding lurched up and moved quickly to the window.

'A buggy,' he barked. 'It's that saloon man.'

Before long, with the buggy secured in the yard and Smith seated in the kitchen, the saloon-owner proffered a broad smile.

'I trust,' he said, 'you all had a good night's rest?'

Stark shook his head. 'Stop the blather, mister. Just tell us what you're playing at!'

Smith, showing no outward sign as worry rose like bile, responded with a nonchalant shrug.

'It worked fine. The sheriff arrested Duggan for the killings and they'll send for a judge.' He sighed and eyed the whiskey on the table. 'You're all in the clear.'

O'Malley thrust the redeye across and shook his head. 'Start talking,' he snarled. 'Why are you helping us?'

Smith shrugged before he reached a hand into his jacket and produced a cloth bag. He lost no time in tipping the contents on to the table, giving a protracted sigh.

They all stared at the tabletop with widened eyes. Out of that bag Smith had delivered a pile of glinting gold nuggets.

'Gold,' Lucas gasped, reaching out with trembling fingers. 'Are these nuggets real?'

'You can count your lives on it,' Smith assured him. 'They're the genuine article, as they say.' He fixed all of them in turn with a piercing glare. 'Fellers, if we can come to some kind of arrangement, what you see on that table is just the start.'

Lucas lifted a nugget and handed it to Stark. The scarfaced murderer stared at it intently before pressing it to his lips. When he lowered it, he had a frenzied look in his eyes.

'These bits,' Stark growled, 'they're out of the Heights?'

'Yeah,' Smith answered. 'They sure are.'

'Well then,' returned Stark with a smirk. 'We definitely *will* be paying those hills a visit before we leave.'

Smith's look darkened. 'I wouldn't call that a good move.' He shook his head. 'Fleet Duggan and two others were the first up there. They panned these bits and then got out fast.' Smith rose to his feet, his features set grim. 'It's sacred ground.'

Stark reached out and took a firm fistful of Smith's jacket. 'Why'd Duggan give you this gold?'

Smith shrugged. 'It was credit for drink.' Smith dragged his jacket out of

Stark's grip. 'This lot's worth a few hundred dollars. I've more gold locked away. I'll top it with cash.'

Stark's eyes narrowed. 'You best start making sense!'

'I said,' snapped Smith testily, 'that I've an arrangement for the right men. If you're the people I need . . . and I reckon you are . . . I'm confident you'll strike a deal.'

A silence followed, laden with wariness.

When Smith spoke again he delivered bitter words.

'I've ached for the deaths of two people.' His eyes, like pools of dark rage, widened. 'One's a woman named Ella Farrell. She and her pa own the livery and live in a house next to it. The other . . . ' He trailed off, his look unreadable.

Stark glared at Smith intently. 'Go on!'

Smith scowled before muttering, 'Stratton's sheriff.'

O'Malley shook his head. 'Are you

crazy, mister? Killing law's a risky deal.' He fixed Smith with a penetrating stare. 'What did this badge do that you'd want his blood so bad?'

Smith drilled his answer through gritted teeth. 'He sent my boy to the gallows.' The saloon-owner stepped towards the door then stopped and looked back. 'Keep those nuggets as down payment. If you kill them both you'll get all the gold and cash as I said.'

'It'll cost,' bellowed Stark as Smith departed to his buggy. 'We want ten thousand.'

The rattle of wheels confirmed Smith's departure. Then, when they all thought he'd gone, his voice returned.

'You'll get all that money when the job's done.'

*   *   *

Sheriff Canning, having checked on the now awake and grumbling Fleet Duggan, stepped back into the jailhouse office to find Ella Farrell standing there.

She eyed him intently before muttering, 'I've just been told.' Her face contorted with distress. 'So Fleet Duggan murdered three men last night?'

Canning shrugged and slid into his chair. 'That's about the stack of it.' He sighed deeply. 'Did Stafford let you know?'

'No,' snapped Ella. 'He's walking about town. I don't reckon to see him until lunchtime.' She pulled out a seat at the opposite side of the desk to Canning and lowered herself into it slowly. 'Young Jack told Pa and that's how I know.'

The sheriff shook his head. 'That boy's got big ears.'

'Jack also said,' muttered Ella slyly, 'that you spoke to Tom about a deputy's post.'

Canning's eyes widened. 'How'd the hell that boy — '

'That doesn't matter,' barked Ella agitatedly. 'What did Tom say?'

'He turned my offer down,' replied

Canning, still annoyed at the local youth's intimate knowledge of everyone's business. 'I tried but he just said no.'

'You've got to persuade him,' Ella blurted, knowing she sounded frantic but unable to suppress the emotion in her voice. 'You've just got to make him stay.'

Canning shrugged. 'What can I do?'

'Go to Mayor Gill,' she pressed urgently. 'Speak to him. Between you you've got to make Tom change his mind.' Ella rose to her feet. 'Promise me you'll do that.'

'I'll think on it,' growled Canning, a little surprised at the intensity of Ella's feeling for Stafford. It had only been a matter of a day since they'd first met.

Ella got to the jailhouse door and glanced back. 'He'll make a fine deputy for Stratton.' She hurried out then, running all the way home to prepare the finest meal for the man she loved.

6

Tom halted his walk and built a smoke. It was now past midday; he'd scoured the entirety of Stratton and mapped the town. The settlement resembled many others: clapboard houses astride gouged-earth roads. Behind the houses ran a network of alleys.

As he'd walked along those passage-ways he'd surprised a few questionable characters: two shifty-looking men in range gear had eyed him sourly as he passed, but neither had spoken. In the next street he'd observed the suspicious behaviour of a man in a battered hat who'd been trying the doorhandles of several properties. The man scurried away when he noticed Tom watching.

At last, with hunger gnawing at his guts, Tom set for Ella's house. Once he'd arrived there, she greeted him with a kiss and showed him into the parlour.

Tom tensed. Another man occupied a seat in there.

'Say,' he exclaimed, glancing sharply at Ella. 'You didn't — '

'This is our mayor, Tom. Now, I'll rustle up coffee and let you fellers talk.'

Ella stepped away. The mayor rose to his feet.

'I'm Carl Gill,' said the mayor with a weak grin. The official resumed his seat and Tom slid into another chair.

'Well, Mr Gill, what do you want with me?'

The mayor frowned. 'You said no to the sheriff?'

Tom nodded. 'I'm not minded to be the law here, or anywhere.'

'No,' intoned Gill drily. 'Ella says you're reluctant to pin on a badge again.'

Tom felt a surge of annoyance. She'd given details of their discussions yesterday and that aggravated him somewhat.

'She meant well,' Gill went on. 'She reckons you're the man we need.' The mayor grimaced. 'Our town's turning bad!'

'You'll always get rough sorts after gold,' returned Tom. 'Or even talk of it.'

'Duggan's slaying of those miners,' Gill drawled. 'I want it to be the last.' The mayor sighed. 'Listen, Stafford, Alf Canning's been a fixture as sheriff but he needs help. I'll appeal to your goodwill and ask you to stay. Take a badge for us.'

Ella's voice sounded then. She'd entered the room unheard, now she placed a tray down.

'I'll plead for you to stay, too. Please stay, Tom. I know you're the man we need. God alive, three men murdered in cold blood!'

'Ella,' Tom groaned. He shaped his lips to say more but she beat him to it.

'I begged the sheriff to ask you.' Her eyes flashed. 'You'd be perfect, Tom. I just know you will.'

'Hear me out please, Stafford,' pressed Gill. 'When you turned down the sheriff's offer, Canning came to me.

He thought I might get you to reconsider.'

'Goddamn it,' said Tom aggrieved. 'I'm just not sure.'

'How can we make you sure?' Gill implored.

Ella walked across. She sat on the arm of Tom's chair and slid a hand into his. 'I'll change his mind. I just know I will.'

* * *

'You reckon we can trust him?'

O'Malley shrugged. 'He's covered your killing of those men and given us this gold and promised us more. We'd be crazy, I reckon, to walk away now.'

Stark picked up the nuggets again. He clutched them in one hand and sniffed at the gold pieces. 'So he's got more, has he?'

'Who'd reckon it?' Lucas said drily. 'That Duggan feller finds gold and gives it over for a few bottles of the hard stuff.'

'No accounting for what folk do,' returned O'Malley. 'Smith's got a grudge as long as the Missouri River. Jeez, he'll give us a fortune to shoot two folk. What a fool bastard.'

Stark's eyes burned maliciously. 'Yeah,' he spat. 'Then we'll blast that saloon man as well.'

They all laughed. Things might work out after all.

*   *   *

Night fell upon all of their lives.

At the farmstead, the four outlaws quaffed the last of the redeye and shared stories of their exploits. It turned into a riotous night, punctuated by laughter. All had relaxed now. Stark kept turning back to the nuggets and holding them like life itself. He'd do anything to retain both.

Sheriff Canning headed home to his wife and they both ate in silence.

Mayor Gill, as he and his wife settled to bed, reassured her that things would improve in Stratton.

In another bed, Tom and Ella nestled together.

'You're not angry are you?' she whispered in his ear.

'Hell, Ella, you should have spoken to me!'

She sighed. 'I know, Tom. Look, I'd do anything to keep you here right now.'

He fell silent and she prodded him with a kiss.

'I told you all about my life,' he said. 'You spoke nothing about your husband.'

'Warren's dead,' she groaned, hurt evident in her voice. 'Like your wife.' She sat up, shaking her head. 'When I found out my world broke. Then, when Fred Smith's boy did the killings, I felt glad.' She gave a sob. 'Afterwards, I just felt sick.'

Tom slid out of the sheets and reached for his clothes. In no time, with a smoke built, he drew long and reflectively.

'I cried when Fred Smith's boy hung,' Ella went on. 'He was so young to die.' She shook her head. 'Since that day, Fred Smith's hated me. I see it in his eyes.'

'What?' Tom growled. 'How can — '

'That's how it is,' she cried. 'Folk were saying it had to be my fault. I'd failed Warren. He wouldn't have gone off if I'd been a better wife.' She sighed and beckoned him back to her side.

He flicked the smoke out of the half-opened window and went to her. Over the time that followed, their longing for each other knew no bounds.

* * *

Under an illuminating moon the Cheyennes rested in their night camp and discussed their options. The twenty-five unwed bucks and the old medicine man Two Moons squatted about a fire. Elsewhere, the few families who accompanied them slept in thrown-up structures of wood and hide. Alienated from the tribe, and on the run, they existed by abiding by the rules of survival.

As the fire's writhing flame cast its light on their exhausted faces, the unwed bucks considered their options. For months, after the US Army had driven them off their ancient lands, they'd fled north. Some of the Cheyenne tribes, they'd heard, had reached Canada. Others, overtaken by the US soldiers or not prepared to fight had submitted to life on the reservations. This band had, with determination, outflanked the harassing cavalry and returned to the southern plains.

'Our ancestors cry for us,' intoned Two Moons in Algonquian. 'They say, go back to the Cheyenne Heights.'

The young bucks stayed silent and sought answers in the flames. They all considered the slaughter on those hills. They'd resisted the US Army onslaught but to no avail. Many blue legs had perished but many brothers as well. How could they, a small band of unproved warriors, succeed against such forces as the white men threw against them.

Two Moons read their thoughts. 'The bluebellies have gone. Now the long beards turn our fathers in their graves. They cast our ancestor's bones from their resting places.'

'Why?' cried out one of the bucks, 'has this happened to us?'

'Blood and gold,' said Two Moons in a tone that chilled their hearts. 'This is the white man's measure of all the earth.' He gestured at another of the bucks.

'What do you say?'

This one shook his head. 'We cannot win, Medicine Father. If we return, what can we do?'

'Kill the long beards,' howled Two Moons. 'Make our ancestors proud and let them sleep in peace again.'

The dissenting buck nodded. 'My own father sleeps at Cheyenne Heights.' The firelight seemed to heighten the hue of his eyes. 'My own father,' he said, recalling a life before the tribe and a pa slain by bandits.

'You are Cheyenne,' spat Two Moons. 'Remember that.'

The white-born man stood up. 'When the sun rises we ride for Cheyenne Heights.' He left and soon the other bucks followed.

Only Two Moons stayed until the flames died. He chanted until dawn carried the extinguished firelight into the sky.

7

O'Malley, stepping out of the farm-house, shielded his eyes with a hand and cast a quick glance upwards.

'Hell,' he muttered. 'It just doesn't let up.'

Above, in the vastness of sky, the sun blazed fiercely. Right now, mid-afternoon, the air baked the plains. That fiery orb burned all: a man's soul if he stood too long, or the vast acres of grass, spanning out on all sides.

When Stark left the building, inhaling deeply on a smoke, he came to stand next to the Irishman. He said nothing for some minutes. At length, though, he spat at the dirt.

'We need more supplies; I need whiskey real bad. I say we set to Stratton and — '

'I've been thinking about that,' cut in O'Malley. He locked Stark with a harsh glare. 'Your face is on a Wanted poster. Lucas's face too. That makes you both a risk. Hell, with the scar, it won't be too long before someone recognizes you.'

Stark dragged out his gun and set the muzzle end between O'Malley's eyes. Quickly though, he reholstered the Schofield and laughed raucously.

'You're just like Lucas — always squawking.' He spun a laughing dance in the yard. 'They can't see me. I'm invisible. I'm the luckiest man in the world!'

'No,' O'Malley muttered as Stark moved into the house. 'You're the goddamn craziest.'

★　★　★

Colonel Parnell Forbes sat his horse on the plains, watching the drummed-up dust of an approaching rider. In no time a sergeant reined up sharply and shook his head.

'They've pitched camp a few miles

71

north-west, sir. We're rounding up the squaws and youngsters about now.' The sergeant shook his head. 'It's dust to the south, sir. Maybe thirty bucks is headed back.'

'Hell's teeth,' spat Forbes. 'We'll escort this lot to the reservation. I want a company to — '

'Begging the colonel's pardon,' cut in the sergeant. 'The men are exhausted. We all need rest.'

Forbes looked up at the vibrant, cloudless sky. The heat was punishing and they hadn't eaten properly for three days. 'The nearest fort's McKay, isn't it?'

'Yeah,' answered the sergeant. 'It's some fifty miles east.'

Forbes nodded. 'We set for there. Rest tonight, Sergeant. Tomorrow though, a company rides south like hell.'

Forbes kicked his horse on, then halted sharply.

'They'll head to the Cheyenne Heights, sir,' the NCO called back. 'Them there miners won't — '

'Yeah,' Forbes growled. 'They won't know what's hit them.'

★　★　★

They let their mounts amble along Main Street. Now, outside the saloon, they eased out of saddles, lashed the horses and then set up the boardwalk steps. Above the Rolling Cloud's batwings, they noted a sign that read: *'Closed for cleaning. Re-open one hour.'*

Inside the deserted hostelry, furiously sweeping the Rolling Cloud's floor, Fred Smith mused on the news. During a walk along Main Street the owner of the saloon had overheard two women talking.

The man who'd shot Fleet Duggan in the foot, one said, was an ex-US marshal called Tom Stafford. He shared, that woman went on, the livery house with Ella and her pa. It also seemed he shared Ella's bed. Finally, as the women stepped away, one of them put forward the belief that Stafford had been invited to take up the deputy's post in Stratton. It was unknown if he'd accepted.

As the batwings clattered, Smith spun and dropped the broom. 'Christ,' he howled, his guts turning. 'You can't be in town.'

Silently, the outlaws slid into chairs.

'Redeye,' Stark growled at last. 'Bring it over.'

Smith grabbed for a bottle. He got there in a hurry and slammed it down. He threw a glance at the batwings.

'You seem sort of jumpy,' drawled Stark, swigging at the redeye. 'What're you fretting about?'

Smith shook his head. 'I thought you'd do this by dark. Jeez, that way you wouldn't be seen.'

Stark's eyes narrowed. A second later, he lurched up with Duggan's purloined Schofield drawn. He pressed the muzzle to Smith's forehead. 'We'll do it when we're good and ready.'

Smith's face drained. 'Sure,' he

spluttered. 'OK.'

Stark bedded the gun and dropped back to his seat.

'We need supplies: liquor, makings, food.' Stark dragged up the Schofield again. 'I want a Colt Peacemaker to replace this piece of iron dirt.'

Smith nodded, trying to appear calm, but his words were urgent. 'Get back to the farm and I'll bring it all soon.'

Stark swigged more whiskey, then got to his feet. The others rose at the same time. As they left, their spurs clanking as they moved, Smith blew out his cheeks in relief. It was short-lived though. Stark halted at the batwings and glared back.

'Your name,' Stark growled. 'Who the hell are you?'

Smith paled. 'I'm Frederick Albert Smith.' He shuddered and said with a gulp, 'And you're . . . ?'

Stark smirked. 'Mister, we're your worst nightmare if you get this wrong.' He nodded and put a hand to the doors. 'Get that stuff to the farm before nightfall. Don't forget the Colt!'

Stark pushed at the batwings but Smith's plaintive wail stilled him.

'We'll let Ella Farrell live,' whined the saloon-owner. 'It's said she's taken up with an ex-marshal. He's the bastard what shot Duggan in the foot.'

Stark, turning again, locked on to Smith with a menacing glare. 'What the hell did you just say?'

'An ex-marshal.' Smith groaned. 'I hear he might hire on as a deputy. Crazy, isn't it? The son of a bitch blasts a man and gets took on as a lawman?'

When none of the outlaws spoke, Smith stepped to the counter and fumbled for a drink. He swallowed a shot glass of redeye and then sucked for air.

'I'd ask that you leave Ella out of this. Just kill Canning for the money agreed.'

Stark scowled. 'You're telling us what to do again.'

'Please,' Smith whined. 'I didn't

76

mean offence. It's just . . . I'll pay the same I offered just to kill Canning. I beg you, forget about Ella — this man called Stafford makes it too risky.'

'Ex-marshal,' Stark growled. He glanced sharply at Lucas. 'And an ex-law that goes by the name of *Stafford*!'

Lucas shook his head. 'You reckon it could be, Cal?'

Stark shrugged. 'It'd be a turn-up and no mistake.'

'You know this ex-marshal?' queried Fielding.

'No, we don't,' muttered Lucas when Stark stayed silent. 'We never met. It's just . . . ' He cast an uncertain look at his partner. 'Cal's brother got gunned down by a marshal with the name of Stafford.'

Stark crashed out of the batwings.

'We'll be waiting,' he yelled from the boardwalk outside. 'Get there before nightfall.'

'Please,' Smith wailed after them, 'you'll leave Ella Farrell alone?'

Smith thought they'd gone but Stark's cruel voice returned.

'No, we'll kill them all just to be sure.'

* * *

The hours slipped past until, with dusk settled over Stratton, Ella poured more coffee and smiled. 'I knew you would.'

Tom frowned. He'd spent the afternoon just sitting in the livery house parlour, thinking deeply on many things. With the meal finished, he resolved to discuss the future. He eyed Ella intently.

'You're mighty sure of yourself, missy.'

'No,' she retorted, running a hand through his hair. 'I'm sure of you.' She grinned again. 'I feel as silly as a first love. Hell, Tom, I think on you from first till last.'

He sipped at the coffee and sighed. 'I can't deny I got strong feelings for you, Ella. Listen, though, getting involved with a badge isn't the best arrangement. A badge means slugs are coming, sooner or later.'

She took a seat opposite him at the table and waved a hand dismissively. 'No two-bit outlaw will get the better of you.'

'That's how it's been up 'til now,' he said softly. 'The trouble is — age slows you. Bit by bit I reckon it'll come.'

'No way,' she retorted. 'You've a heck of years on Sheriff Canning and you're all the man I need.'

He climbed to his feet and slid on his Stetson. 'I'm headed to talk to Canning and Mayor Gill. I'm not sure if they'll want me to start straight away.'

She nodded. 'Whatever time you get back I'll be waiting.'

He left then, stepping outside and descending the boardwalk steps beneath the rapidly darkening sky. The light of lamps sparkled behind windows; the dull thump of piano music sounded from further down the street, and men's raucous laughter carried on that evening's slightest breeze.

He gazed up and saw a moon starting to rise. He considered the silvery edge and knew that soon stars would be pinpoints of white. Two of those were his wife and child.

'Don't be angry with me,' he whispered as he walked. 'I love you both but I've got to keep living.' He stopped and stifled a sob. He recalled the discussion with his slain wife shortly after they'd married. If something happened — if one of them died — the other would never wed again.

'Lorna,' Tom whispered as he neared the jail. 'I'm struggling to keep that pledge!'

8

In the blackness of the enfolding night, Fred Smith flicked the buggy's reins and kept the team of two moving steadily. He'd delivered the provisions as agreed and now, heading back to town, he crossed a landscape cloaked in darkness. He cursed as he drove, wondering whether the man he'd left in charge of the saloon would cope or what the clientele would make of it. They'd question his absence, for sure. If word of that got to Sheriff Canning it might prove to be awkward.

Smith sighed and mused uneasily on Ella Farrell. Sure, his hatred for her knew no bounds, but to try to kill her now with this ex-marshal so close was utter madness. Even so, and despite repeated pleading when he'd got to the farmstead, that scarfaced maniac remained resolved. He'd slay them all.

Later, closing on Stratton's western lights, Smith's guts lurched. He'd lost control of the unstoppable train of vengeance he'd set in motion. These four men — these nameless, shady thugs — would visit terror on the streets of Stratton. They'd inflict a carnage for which they held Smith to account. No matter what Smith or anyone else in the world said or did, there'd be a bloodletting in this settlement.

* * *

In the jailhouse, Mayor Gill shook Tom's hand. 'Goddamn it,' he said. 'That's right pleasing news.'

Tom, extracting himself from the official's sustained grip, nodded at Canning.

'You've got a badge for me?'

Canning opened a drawer in his desk and produced a tin star. He grinned before stepping across and pinning it to Tom's vest.

'You can swear in later, Stafford. Right now we'll take a drink.' The sheriff quickly dispensed whiskey and they shared a toast. 'I'm sure,' said Canning then, 'that with the two of us we'll stamp down on thugs. We'll get this business with Fleet Duggan settled and eliminate trouble before it starts.'

Tom nodded. He was just setting the shot glass to his lips when he heard a clatter on the boardwalk. Soon, a man hurried into the jail.

'Sheriff, we've got a ruckus at the saloon.'

Canning reached for his rifle. 'Well, Tom,' he observed, 'it looks like your first duty is right now!'

Tom got his Colt to hand. 'Listen, Sheriff, and no offence, but now I'm deputy you don't go charging into situations alone. You said yourself you're getting on.'

The flash of anger in Canning's eyes dissipated fast. He smiled. 'OK, I'll wait for you before tackling stuff.'

Leaving Mayor Gill in the law office,

83

they crossed to the saloon. Inside the Rolling Cloud, busy with night drinkers, a man prodded a pistol at the bartender's chest. Quickly though, seeing Tom and Canning push through the batwings, he lowered the gun and slid it to a holster.

'Mister,' Canning growled, 'why'd you draw your piece on that barkeep?'

The man fixed Canning with a searching glare.

'I'm Leyton Wavering. I mined up at Cheyenne Heights with Fleet Duggan a time back.'

Canning shrugged. 'That gives you the right to shove a gun at a man, does it?'

Wavering frowned. 'That barkeep says Fleet's in jail for murder. Hell no, for the murder of *three* men.'

'That's right,' snapped Canning. 'I have to say, mister, that's due process of law; it don't give you a right to threaten nobody.'

'Where's Fred Smith?' Wavering spat.

Canning frowned. 'Yeah, where is

he?' he muttered. He anchored the man behind the counter with an inquisitive glare. 'Why are you tending beer, Deacon Fuller?'

'Smith asked me to,' growled Fuller. He shrugged. 'I've helped out before, you know that!'

Canning grunted and set his gaze back to Wavering.

'You've got a couple of choices: ride out and stay free, or else carry this on and be in a cell next to your pal Duggan.'

'You know that Fred Smith fleeced Duggan?' Wavering barked, undeterred. 'You know Fleet's slow in thinking — backward, your fancy doctors would say? Fleet likes his redeye and that there saloon man wheedles Fleet's gold nuggets for a handful of shots and the promise of more liquor.'

'You saying Smith defrauded Duggan?' questioned Tom.

Wavering snorted. 'Defraud? All I know is that Fleet and Smith got as thick as molasses. Sure, Fleet's a bully, but that big woodenhead wouldn't kill a fly.'

'He threatened me,' grunted Tom.

'I don't know,' Wavering spat. 'God-damn it, something's not right.' He grabbed his hat off the bar and strode to the batwings. 'They'll hang Fleet but you got to keep an eye on Smith. He can't be trusted and that's that!'

When Wavering had gone the saloon's atmosphere lightened fast. With talk swelling about the room, Tom and Sheriff Canning took their departure, then paused on the boardwalk outside.

Tom shrugged. 'I'd be obliged to start my first shift in the morning. Tonight, well, you know where I am if needed?'

Canning nodded. 'Sure. You've got something planned?'

'Ella,' said Tom. 'Things are moving at a pace.'

Canning watched Tom stride away. He stepped to the street himself then, musing on retirement all the way to the jail.

* * *

Two men exchanged punches outside the shack saloon on Cheyenne Heights but Eli Flint's attention lay elsewhere. He listened with fascination and horror to the discussion of two men. Mining finished for the day and that night's highland darkness kept at bay by kerosene lamps, the shantytown shook with noise and anger. With finds made, aggressive envy had become palpable.

'Goddamn it,' spat one miner. 'I heard good nuggets got found today. The man what struck them rode straight away.'

'This is no good,' growled back another. 'All the best stuff is took before I get to it. I'm headed Dakota way.'

'You're crazy. You wouldn't put a foot in them Black Hills. I heard Indians are thereabouts; you'll be scalped or worse.'

'Huh . . . Indians you say? We dug up a heck of bones today. I threw them out for the critters.'

Eli shook his head. 'I don't reckon

you should be shifting the dead,' he offered earnestly. 'It don't sound good, that.'

'Go to hell. I'll shift Indians dead or alive.'

Eli grabbed a bottle and took a swig. Outside, the fistfight ended. Laughter and curses rent the air.

'God alive,' Eli sighed as he quaffed more whiskey. They'd dug up graves. It didn't need a genius to work out what that might mean.

★　★　★

They sat in the lounge as writhing flames danced their orange performance upon red-hot coals.

'You sure look good with that badge pinned on,' said Stanley Farrell with a grin. 'It's Deputy Sheriff Stafford, eh?'

'I start in the morning,' responded Tom, sipping at a glass of brandy that Ella had proffered. 'Listen,' he said. 'I'll pay my way. So long as I'm stopping here I'll give board and such.'

Stanley shrugged. 'There's no need, Deputy!'

'I want to. I want — '

'No,' cut in Ella. 'You're being here's our gift.'

They were in adjacent high-backed chairs. Tom put aside his glass and gripped her hand. 'You've been so good to me.'

'I knew the moment I saw you,' she said firmly, 'that you were what Stratton needed.' She had a glint in her eye. 'And that means all of us that live here.'

'I'll do my best with this badge,' he said.

She smiled but stayed silent. Tom stared into the flames of the open fire and pondered how he'd tell her. No matter how long he stayed here, no matter how close they got, he couldn't break that pledge to his dead wife. He and Ella could never wed!

9

As the light of a new day flooded the windows, Stark smoked and pondered on Cheyenne Heights.

'We can't leave without checking those hills,' he growled at length. 'God alive, they must be loaded with gold.'

Lucas couldn't disguise a groan. He shook his head, his eyes wide and filled with disquiet.

'Cal? You heard what Smith said: that's sacred Injun land. I'd not reckon — '

'Shut it,' bellowed Stark. 'You're squawking again.'

'No,' interjected Fielding then. 'Sure, we set here for gold but things have changed. That saloon man's money is enough. We'll do his bidding for the dollars he'll pay. I'll not go on sacred Cheyenne land.'

'Jeez,' Stark spat. 'You'd let a few old

wives' tales keep you from a fistful of nuggets?'

'Old wives' tales?' barked Fielding. 'Mister, we've ridden against the tribes and we know what they can do. I'll not risk it when we can get what we want in town.' He shook his head. 'Hell, think about it; if Smith can pay ten grand then he's got to have more.' He threw a frantic look at O'Malley. 'You'll back me on this, Pat?'

O'Malley sighed. 'I don't know. It's said those Cheyennes have gone north. If it's true we can't let this chance go.'

Fielding looked aghast. 'Damn it, Pat, you've seen what Cheyenne braves make of a man when they're riled?'

O'Malley slapped his partner on the shoulder. 'Stay it, Lee, those Cheyennes have gone. It'll be OK.'

Stark anchored Lucas with a withering glare. 'And you?'

Lucas gulped. 'We're partners, aren't we? If you say we go then that's how it is!'

Stark smirked. 'We'll set to Stratton

and do the killings. Once Smith's paid up we'll kill him and set to those hills.'

O'Malley started to build a smoke.

'Say, Stark,' he said, 'this here ex-marshal — why'd he kill your kid brother?'

Stark shrugged. 'Zane jumped a store at Cedarville, Missouri. This Stafford gunned my baby brother down right between the eyes.' Stark's look darkened. 'Zane was just twenty-one.'

O'Malley nodded. 'Revenge will taste good when you blast this ex-marshal, then?'

'No,' Stark growled back. 'I already had revenge.' He looked at them slyly. 'I shared a cell in Nebraska with this man, name of Garfield. As mad as you'd get, he was. He'd rave and such to make you sleep with one eye open. Garfield got out a year before me. He promised to go to Cedarville and kill Stafford.'

O'Malley inhaled on his smoke. 'He failed you, then?'

'No,' gave back Stark crossing the room and reaching for a whiskey bottle.

'Stafford weren't there.'

O'Malley shrugged. 'Bad luck then?'

'No,' repeated Stark icily. 'But his wife and bitch kid were. Garfield blasted them.'

A fraught silence ensued. Fielding broke it.

'Your man killed this marshal's child?'

'I heard the cur kid were about six or such,' Stark said. 'Garfield blasted her in the head.'

Stark stepped out of the shack, leaving O'Malley and Fielding struck dumb. They both cast imploring looks at Lucas but he turned away.

For the two ex-soldiers, one thing emerged with clarity: when this was over, they'd get away from Stark as fast as they could.

* * *

In one of the cells of Stratton jailhouse, Tom watched as the town's physician Ralph Warner rebandaged Fleet Duggan's foot. Once he'd finished tending to the prisoner the physician stood up and washed his hands in a bowl. He studied the town's new deputy sheriff with a piercing stare.

'It's a peculiarity of Judge Del Mar,' he growled. 'He won't hang a sick or injured man. No, sir, a man's got to be fighting fit before he can get hung.'

Behind him, seated on the bunk, Fleet Duggan gulped.

The doctor left and Tom sighed. 'It's a sorry business.'

'What the hell do you care?' Duggan snarled. 'I've been in a heck of a lot of pain on account of your slug.'

'You slapped Mrs Farrell.'

Duggan shrugged. 'That was my last four dollars. I was waiting for Smith to give me more money.'

Tom frowned. 'How many nuggets did you give that man?'

Duggan looked down. 'A few thousand dollars' worth, I'd reckon. I messed up. It's just . . . I need the liquor.'

'Try arguing you were drunk,' suggested Tom. 'It might not save you, but you've got nothing to lose.'

Duggan's face broke. He held his head in his hands and emitted a deep and protracted sob. 'They'll hang me and I didn't kill those men.' He looked up again, eyes wide and fearful. 'I was drunk, mister, but I didn't do it.'

Tom shrugged. 'You've no witnesses. From what the sheriff says, it was just you in the saloon with them miners. Smith was out back and heard you arguing before the shooting.'

Duggan, wincing with pain, struggled to his feet.

'No,' he said firmly. 'There were other men there. They came in late, and then I can't recall any more.'

Tom's interest began to stir. 'What's that?'

'Like I said,' growled Duggan. 'It was late and I was kicked by the liquor. I couldn't tell you what they looked like sure enough but for one feller.' Duggan raised a finger to the right side of his chin. 'A dog scarred for life he was.' Duggan sat back down and considered the newly applied bandage. Looking up again, he groaned as Deputy Stafford plunged out of the cell.

★ ★ ★

With the troops halted, Colonel Forbes took his bearings. He glanced across at his sergeant.

'I'd reckon maybe sixty miles back to the Heights.'

The sergeant nodded. 'A couple of days' ride.'

Forbes scowled. 'You reckon them Cheyennes will take that?'

'No, sir,' snorted the NCO. 'I'd reckon they'll do distances in one day that'd break most men and horses. Begging the colonel's pardon, we could try the same but, get to the other end, we won't have the strength to fight.'

Forbes shook his head. 'I know it. Still, we have to set a hard pace.'

The sergeant gave a resigned shrug. 'We'll ride the best we can, sir.'

'Them there miners,' said Forbes

sombrely. 'They've got mad-as-hell Cheyennes headed at them and they haven't got a clue.'

The NCO said nothing but his eyes seemed to advise caution.

'Horses, ho!' yelled the colonel then. 'Move out.'

★　★　★

Smith threw down a hand towel as the batwings creaked. He fixed Stratton's newly appointed deputy with a scathing look.

'They say any can get on,' he growled, 'if their face fits.'

'We need to talk,' returned Tom, unfazed. He stepped up to the counter and slid off his Stetson. 'A redeye would be welcome.'

Smith's look darkened but he dispensed the drink. He shoved it across the counter top with a grunt.

'Now,' said Tom, sipping the whiskey and letting the burn settle in his guts. 'Fleet Duggan's talked some.'

Smith shrugged. 'He's a drunk; he's always talking!'

'Duggan swears he wasn't in here alone when those miners died.' Tom fixed Smith with a penetrating glare. 'You want to answer on that?'

Smith shook his head. 'Duggan *is* crazy. I already told Canning. There was only Fleet and those old miners in the saloon. I was out back and . . . ' Smith trailed off and cursed loudly. 'What's the point? I said how it was!'

'A man with a scar,' Tom pressed. 'What about him?'

'You listen to me,' snapped Smith. 'I haven't got a clue what you're talking about. There was no one here except Fleet Duggan and them dead miners.' Smith's face contorted to a sneer. 'You'd best wise up. I know you marshalled at some place East but the facts about this town is that Duggan's a drunkard, a violent fool, and he slaughtered three men for nothing. That's the end of it.'

Tom finished the whiskey and proffered a coin.

'Keep your money,' said Smith. 'I
always oil the law.'

Tom nodded and strode towards the
doors. He chucked the coin over his
shoulder as he went through the
batwings. It clattered on the floor and
he stood rigidly still on the boardwalk.

'You hear me, Deputy?' bellowed
Smith. 'I oil the law. Don't you be like
that bastard Canning! Don't be like
him, Stafford! You're a dog barking up
the wrong tree!'

10

After securing their horses in a quiet street at the edge of town, they navigated a foot-route through the alleyways. Those whom they passed along the way — folk with suspicion in their eyes — said nothing and hurried away.

Now, obscured in the shadows, they tracked the passage of traffic along Main Street. The boardwalks creaked under the weight of numbers — ordinary people sauntering between stores or just mooching over the walkway rails. Along the scarred dirt road wagons trundled in line between a legion of mounted riders, either setting into town or leaving.

Yet, in that hive of activity, Lucas spotted something and he jabbed out with his hand.

'There,' he hissed. 'You reckon that's Stafford?'

Stark locked his gaze on to one man. In the centre of Main Street, stepping aside to let a wagon pass, a man bearing a star on his vest doffed his Stetson before walking on.

Stark's eyes narrowed. 'Yeah.' He spat. 'That'll be him, sure enough.' His hand slipped to his gun but O'Malley stilled him.

'No,' the Irishman growled. 'We've got to plan this.'

Stark's eyes blazed but he quelled his fury.

'OK,' he growled. 'What do we do?'

'Just wait,' cautioned O'Malley, 'for *his* next move.'

When it came — Tom stepping through the flung-open doors of the livery — O'Malley gave a decided nod.

'Now.' The Irishman spat. 'We'll get it done.'

Stark grinned and dragged a blade from his belt. 'This way nothing's heard.'

Lucas muttered a low curse. In nearly three decades of crime, he'd once hit a man with a coal poker during a robbery gone wrong. He'd avoided slaying at any cost. The taking of life — or so it seemed to Lucas's reckoning — was an unnecessary extreme that could be avoided.

Caleb Stark — as his actions had shown since Lucas had met the man — operated at the other end of the violence spectrum.

Now, with disquiet gnawing at Lucas's guts, he followed the others as they came out of the alley and merged into the crowd of people clogging the boardwalk. Soon, swallowed into that shifting mass of bodies, they moved unnoticed towards the saloon.

When they closed upon the Rolling Cloud, Stark hissed out his plan.

'Me and O'Malley will get this done. Lucas, you and Fielding stay outside. If that deputy shows you know what to do?'

Quickly then, Stark and O'Malley pushed through the batwings. Fielding fixed Lucas with a sombre look.

'I've met some crazy sons of bitches in my time,' he grumbled, 'but Stark's up there with the worst.' He shook his head. 'What'd make a man that way?'

Lucas shrugged. 'Some are like that,' he answered sonorously. 'They're plain evil from birth to grave!'

★ ★ ★

'So you reckon he's lying?'

Tom, having rapidly consumed the lunch Ella had served, pushed aside the plate.

'I just don't know,' he said. 'That Fred Smith's got a heck of an anger about him, sure enough.'

'Mostly for me,' she answered morosely. 'And of course — '

'Sheriff Canning,' completed Tom, 'on account of he saw to the hanging of Smith's boy.'

Ella stood behind him and nestled her head against his. 'This man with the scar,' she said. 'Why's he so important — if it was the same man, of course.'

Tom stood up and embraced her. 'I killed his brother. Stark would want my blood, sure enough.'

'But, Tom,' exclaimed Ella with passion. 'You said yourself that it's years ago. There isn't a chance it's this man called Stark.'

'Duggan wasn't lying, Ella,' he said softly. 'A man with a scar on his face killed those three miners. I can't say it's Stark but it sure as hell could be.'

'And Smith's involved?'

Tom shrugged. 'He knows what it's about but won't talk.'

'Of course he wouldn't,' she returned. 'He gets in league with bad men and it'd cost him his life.'

'Ella,' said Tom sternly, 'until I get a hold of what's going on I want you and your pa to stay about the livery.'

Her eyes flashed. 'Don't you be telling me — '

He stilled her with a kiss. 'I'm not telling, I'm asking.' He sighed and crossed the room. 'I'll talk with Canning.'

'I want to marry you, Tom Stafford.'

He stopped and cursed under his breath. He lowered his head and fought the bile that rose in his throat.

'Did you hear what I said?'

'I love you,' he whispered as he stumbled out.

★ ★ ★

Eli Flint, drawn by an unusual sound, stepped out of the shack. He shook his head and scanned the deserted shanty-town. Save for a few who were nursing injuries and were inside their huts, all the miners were toiling that day. Flint scratched at his head. Hell, that sound had made his guts lurch. It was — or so his instinct told him — the noise a man makes in violent death. He shuddered and turned back to his shack.

He froze, bile touching his throat. That gut-wrenching cry sounded again — a howl of such unimaginable agony that it sickened Eli from the pit of his stomach. He lurched into the shack and grabbed his shotgun. When he got outside again he moved with tentative steps.

Now he stumbled, his legs buckling under him and a gasp escaping his lips. Close by, three Indians gripped a man called Markham. While one buck pinned Markham's arms, the others drew knife blades across the miner's face.

Fighting against his terror, Eli levelled the shotgun and fumbled a finger to the trigger. He held back from firing, though. Markham's ongoing torture snared Eli's eyes. He watched, with sickened disquiet, as the knives worked open wounds to reveal bloody depths of flesh. So horrifyingly enthralled had he become, in fact, that he was quite unaware of the Cheyenne buck at his back. He felt the press of cold, hard metal to his throat. Then there was eternal nothingness.

★ ★ ★

Canning, pondering agitatedly on when Stafford would show after lunch, continued to monitor the two men slouched over the boardwalk rail by the saloon. The sheriff sighed. A few minutes before, despite the number of people filling the boardwalks, he'd observed two more rough looking characters entering the Rolling Cloud. The fact that he didn't recognize any of the four wasn't unusual these days, given the number of strangers flooding the town.

Canning glanced at the clock repeatedly before, sighing, he made up his mind. He reached for his Colt. He thought back to his promise to Stafford, then he dismissed it. Hell, hadn't he, Alf Canning kept law in Stratton for over two decades? No, this would be fine. He'd speak to these four incomers and question their purpose in town. With that, sliding on his hat, he strode out into the sunshine and crossed the street.

Once he'd traversed the rutted-earth

thoroughfare, Canning took the board-walk steps at a jog before halting outside the saloon doors. Despite the noise of Main Street, he could detect raised voices from within the Rolling Cloud. He shook his head and glanced at two men who were hugging the rail.

'You boys just hit town?'

Fielding bristled, hurriedly thinking up some alias should the sheriff request a name. Fielding stood straight then, his look made brave. 'Just a trail rest, then we're headed out again.'

Canning jabbed his hand at the batwings. 'You're with them two in there?'

Fielding shrugged. 'It's only me and my buddy here. Sorry, Sheriff, I haven't a clue who you're talking about.'

Canning sensed the man lied, but it would have to wait. More shouts sounded from inside the Rolling Cloud — bellowed, curse-littered invective — and he'd deal with that first. After-wards, he'd press these drifters outside about their mission in town. With his mind decided, the sheriff spat at the planks, spun angrily on his heel and eased through the batwings of the Rolling Cloud.

Canning faltered fast. There, inside the saloon, he looked upon shocking violence. The balding Fred Smith, his face pale and his eyes filled with terror, had a knife pressed to his neck. The man who wielded the blade — one of the pair Canning had seen entering earlier — turned sharply and fixed the sheriff with a piercing glare.

Canning's guts lurched. Fred Smith's assailant — a scarred creature with vicious eyes — radiated an aura of evil.

'What the hell?' Canning gasped. 'Mister, I'd — '

His words choked off as Stark, loosing the knife, lunged for his gun.

Canning, with his favoured Winchester rifle locked in the jail, relied now on the speed of his draw. He dropped a hand to his Colt's butt but achieved no more. With his fingers inching off his gun, he watched, transfixed, as the scarface levelled his own weapon.

Stark smirked and shook his head. 'Jeez,' he laughed. 'The goddamn turkey's walked itself to dinner.'

Canning, sick with fear, parted his lips to beg. He didn't get to plead, though. Stark's Colt bellowed and a slug ripped through smoke and cordite to slam into the sheriff's guts. He fell before Stark's gun roar had died. Slumping to his knees, hands clawing hopelessly at a gaping wound, he crashed down on the Rolling Cloud's boards. He lay face down in the sawdust, blood spreading about his still, dead form.

'There,' growled Stark. He jabbed his still-smoking pistol at Smith. 'We did the job. Now you'll pay up, dog!'

Smith sobbed. 'It's in the safe out back.'

Stark cursed and hauled Smith towards the bar. He paused though, musing on the faces peering in over the batwings. They soon disappeared — another gun blast sending those few emboldened onlookers diving for cover.

Outside the saloon, as locals scattered, Fielding and Lucas scurried for cover. They hunkered down by a rain barrel as the street cleared — people running into doorways or into the alleys. Before long, Main Street settled to silence, Fielding hauled up his gun and inched toward the batwings.

Reluctantly now, Lucas followed. They inched on, getting to within feet of the swing doors before the batwings crashed and they dived to the boards. Both knelt now, their guns levelled, watching aghast as O'Malley came out fast through the batwings.

'Jeez, Pat,' spat Fielding. 'What's going on?'

O'Malley's eyes sparked. 'The sheriff's dead. When Stark's got the dollars we ride.'

Fielding frowned. 'And the Farrell woman and that marshal?'

O'Malley shook his head. 'We get our shares and we're out of here.' He jabbed his gun in the direction of the livery. 'That man Stafford won't be long in coming.' He lurched round and yelled into the saloon, 'Get it done fast, Stark, for all our sakes!'

Now they waited anxiously on the boardwalk for Stark to show. Time dragged by — a passage of minutes but it seemed like for ever. Each moment, in their perception, had stretched itself; each ticking second was slowed and clogged by their fears.

They all mused silently on the same thing: if they succeeded in this, they'd leave this town as rich and winning men. Yet, in a roused town after the slaying of a sheriff, nothing was certain. The most peaceable people fought back. Fail and they'd perish. Get caught and they'd swing.

When Stark still hadn't showed each of them fought the urge to flee. The lure of money kept them anchored there. They all knew, though, how fragile was the balance. It was cotton-thread thin — that fine line between triumph and death.

11

Despite his reservations, Colonel Forbes had driven his men hard and they'd neared to within a few hours' ride of the hills. Now he barked for a halt, and the cavalry detail reined up. Holding in the saddle, the assorted troopers watched the roll of dust with growing unease.

Forbes, worry turning his guts, dragged field glasses out of his saddle-bag and scanned the distance. Then he slid the glasses back and fixed his NCO with a grim stare.

'Indians,' he muttered. 'They've gotten the jump on us.' He shook his head. 'We'll ride for cover.'

They moved fast, dragging their mounts about and plunging into the distance. With horses urged into gallops, they thundered on, but Forbes soon realized they couldn't sustain the pace. Already, some of the men had fallen behind as their mounts succumbed to exhaustion. Jabbing a hand at a creek bed, Forbes ordered a stand-to.

They dismounted and lashed reins at speed, before each trooper made for a shooting spot. That dried-out water route offered ideal cover: wide, high banks, colonized by scrub. They'd cover aplenty, but had they the guts and slugs?

A young private faltered first.

'Jeez,' he wailed. 'It don't matter a pig in dirt about nothing now. We'll all die this day.'

'Stay that talk,' roared Forbes. 'I'll have the next man who whines shot where he is.'

A tension-filled quiet settled then, broken eventually by the drumming intensity of the Indians' galloping approach. When they showed — some two dozen Cheyennes on painted ponies — their howling warnings froze blood in the veins.

In time, the Cheyennes stilling their cries and bringing their mounts into a line, silence settled over those plains.

Time laboured then — slow, introspective moments to consider how you'll die. They'd all heard the tales but most dismissed them in a redeye haze. Right here, sober and with Cheyennes close, each man changed his mind.

When the Cheyennes didn't attack — their stilled rank maintained through those dragging, stress-stretched minutes, men began to crack. Forbes himself, his nerve frayed to breaking-point, forced his head against the creek bank and uttered a curse.

'You heathens,' he cried. 'Any of you bastards speak our lingo and hear that?'

A voice returned — speaking in English and without a hint of accent. 'I hear you, bluelegs.'

Forbes lurched up and scrambled out of the creek.

'What're you doing?' barked the NCO. 'Are you crazy, sir?'

Forbes, ignoring his startled sergeant's cry, strode on to the plain and advanced steadfastly towards the Cheyenne line. When he got there, he gazed with great interest at one of those bucks. An Indian with blond hair and blue eyes meant only one thing.

Forbes shook his head. 'You got took, mister?'

The blond buck nodded. 'I am Cheyenne.'

'Hell,' spat Forbes. 'These savages killed your folks?'

'No,' said the blond man testily. 'My family were shot by white men. The Cheyenne helped me. They are my family now.' His eyes flashed. 'Our ancestors call for revenge.'

Forbes shook his head. 'I couldn't stop people going to Cheyenne Heights. I respect your sacred ground.'

The blond man's eyes narrowed. He yelled out in Algonquian and the other bucks erupted into a howling chant. When that subsided, the blond hair fixed Forbes with a fierce glare.

'We give you life today.'

Forbes spat at the grass. 'I've got orders. I have to protect those miners and drive you people off your land.'

'No,' said the blond man icily. He turned his pony and jabbed a hand at the hills. 'I let you leave. Stay and die.'

Later, when the dust of the departed Cheyennes had settled, Forbes stood on the baked grass with his head bowed.

* * *

Tom had his Colt drawn as the first gun bellowed. Now, in the middle of Main Street, he watched dismayed as panic gripped the people. Stratton's populace, fleeing their cover, rushed towards him from all sides. Soon, folk converging at pace, it seemed that they all had the same purpose in mind: get close to the law. Jeez, Tom mused angrily, it was as if the badge now pinned on his chest signified some omnipotent ability to keep slugs at bay.

He stilled his fury and took control.

As the locals hurtled nearer, he directed them past the livery and out towards the edge of town. As they passed many muttered the information Tom sought.

The shooting came from the saloon, one woman cried. Sheriff Canning, another man gasped, had entered the Rolling Cloud alone. Not long after, those gun blasts had sounded.

With the street cleared, Tom shuddered and blanked the notion that Stratton's sheriff might be dead. He scanned the thoroughfare and thought fast. He sighted them then: three men gathered on the boardwalk outside the saloon. Involved or not, Tom decided, they'd be apprehended and questioned.

He moved fast. He got to the boardwalk and took the steps at a leap. Up on the planks, he ducked down behind a tower of crates. There was cover enough all the way to the saloon — sacks and boxes stacked perfectly for shooting sites.

Squatting now and checking his .45, Tom pondered sombrely on Sheriff Alf

Canning. God alive, what had the man done? The warning had been clear: *Don't tackle anything alone.*

Tom spat at the timbers. Blame needed to wait.

Canning, if he still lived, required help fast.

Upright now, his gun to hand, Tom inched along the boardwalk. He soon dived for cover again. The two men standing at the saloon doors had turned, their gazes now directed along the street. Cursing, but sure he hadn't been seen, Tom hazarded a peek around the stack of boxes he hid behind.

His look confirmed it. One of the trio paced distractedly, his head down. Those two with guns had turned back to the batwings; both were staring now into the saloon.

Tom grabbed his chance. He sucked in air and got fast to his feet. He strode on, traversing the walkway at a steady pace. He walked resolutely. There'd be no more hides or cover sites. From here to the saloon he'd complete each step in the open.

He ran then, hurtling across the distance with his footfalls pounding the boards. That slapping echo off the timbers soon alerted those he neared.

O'Malley jerked round and sighted him first.

'Look at that,' he growled. 'My God, he's got guts!'

The Irishman spat and dragged up his gun. He slammed a finger at the trigger and then spat a curse. His .45 jerked in his hand, a bullet leaving the muzzle through flame and smoke. When the bullet struck, biting splinters out of a post, O'Malley cursed. He'd missed the approaching lawman by inches.

Tom ducked as the slug whipped past his ear, then gasped his relief. He faltered though, halted his run and levelled his gun. Then he dropped as more bullets shredded the air.

Panicked and angry, both O'Malley and Fielding loosed bullets fast. Soon, slugs were scything about that board-walk and keeping Tom pinned down as he pressed his face to the timbers and willed himself to survive.

Hell came to Stratton in a cacophony of noise. Gun blasts echoed, roars and bullets shrieked about the street. The sounds of damage were audible now — a slug from Fielding slamming into a window and bringing it down in a cascade of crashing glass. A shot from O'Malley got close, ripping into the boards close by Tom's right leg. As splinters bucked out of the struck timbers, Tom howled at the stab of pain in his foot. A quick look showed it all: inch-long slivers of wood had arrowed through the leather of his boot. His pierced foot ached like hell and he gritted his teeth against the hurt. He got to his knees, cursing loudly and loosing slugs of his own.

The Colt barked in his grip, the bullets screeching through the baked day's air to smash into an awning-post close by the saloon. Tom howled in agony and anger. He'd missed those men but his wayward aim had delivered results.

The trio bolted, all plunging through the Rolling Cloud's swing doors. Now, with the walkway his, Tom got back to his feet and struggled onward. Fury coursed through him and he limped towards the saloon. He'd get to the wounded Sheriff Canning, no matter what it took.

A man possessed, some said of Tom Stafford when he closed upon his prey, as if the man blanked out the world and focused only on the criminals he sought. As if offering proof enough, Tom stumbled now in oblivion, acknowledging nothing — not the blood gushing from his ankle or those pitiful wails pursuing him along the boards.

If he'd turned to look he'd have witnessed the struggle outside the livery. Stanley Farrell, grapling with his deranged daughter, summoned all his strength and kept her restrained.

At last, giving up the fight, Ella sank to her knees and sobbed uncontrollably between screamed-out pleas.

'No, Tom.' Her cries resounded. 'Don't die on me. Oh, sweet Jesus, get away from there!'

* * *

Stark spat furiously as the others crashed into the saloon.

'Hell's teeth,' he barked. 'It sounds like a goddamn war out there.' He waggled a canvas bag in one hand whilst his other gripped Smith's shirt. 'We got us a first-rate payday, boys.'

'Hell we have,' O'Malley bellowed. He spun about and covered the swing doors with his Colt. 'That lawman Stafford's pinned us in.'

Fielding spun to face the door and levelled his gun. 'It's nothing but a stinking mess, I'd say.'

Lucas staggered to the counter and grabbed for a bottle.

'Oh, no,' he muttered after swigging

long of the redeye. 'I don't want to end my days in this two-bit town.'

Stark's eyes narrowed. 'He's but one man. There's four of us.' He locked Lucas with a scathing look. 'Get a grip on that pistol, mister, or so help me I'll blast you where you stand.'

Reluctantly, his eyes screaming no, Lucas drew the Colt strapped to his right leg and shakily thumbed back the hammer.

Stark nodded, resolutely. 'Right, boys, we've got us twenty thousand dollars and more nuggets on top. I don't intend to lose this much booty, no matter what's outside.'

Smith continued to struggle against the scarface's grip. 'You bastard,' he cried. 'You'll ruin me.'

'You're a goddamn fool,' scoffed Stark. 'Your first mistake was not shoving that gold in a bank. Your second was doing a deal with us.

'Please,' Smith wailed. 'You've got the money; let me live?'

Stark's eyes flashed menacingly. He

stuffed the bag inside his shirt and grabbed Smith by the collar. He jabbed the muzzle end of his Colt at the saloon owner's left eye. 'I'll blast you where you stand and paint your own goddamn walls.'

'Oh, for the love of God,' howled Smith. 'Please, I beg you, let me live.'

'Hell, Stark,' growled O'Malley. 'What'll we do?'

'Leave,' said Stark curtly, 'and this dog's our ticket out.'

* * *

Tom's leg buckled and he dropped to one knee, his gun arm raised and his Colt trained towards the saloon. Now, though, the pain in his foot overwhelmed him. That searing ache in his limb raged and Tom glanced down to see blood spreading out on the boards. He growled and defied the agony. A swamp of dizziness almost brought him down but he steadied himself. He half-turned then, noticing a voice calling out from close behind him.

'Deputy,' an old man bellowed from a doorway. 'Didn't you hear what Missy Farrell said?'

Tom shook his head. 'No,' he gasped. He struggled to utter it, the nausea that flooded his body growing stronger by the moment. 'What?'

'Retreat, you crazy son of a bitch.' The old man shook his head. 'The truth is you're not taking out that many men.'

Tom cursed against his failure and weakness. He cursed against the tragedy that had destroyed his life. He finally cursed against his love for Ella.

Her wails came to him, carried on the slightest of breezes.

'Tom, get here to the livery for pity's sake!'

He began to move back, manoeuvring between cover and feeling the life draining out of him until he had to struggle to move. When he passed out — or so it seemed — a wave of darkness engulfed him on that day-lit street.

When he awoke, he was on the floor of one of the stores, with people peering down at him.

An old woman shook her head. 'He'll mend,' she cackled. 'I'll see to that.'

* * *

'Begging your pardon, sir,' muttered a trooper, 'but what in hell's name are we set to do?'

Palls of smoke rose over a farmstead and all of them knew what that meant. Cheyennes had wiped the place out. A heck of a lot of people slaughtered. Colonel Forbes recited an unheard prayer. He hoped they'd died swiftly. They'd all heard tales of unimaginable torture and could only pray that death had come swiftly for the folk there.

Forbes sighed. 'If we set to those hills the Cheyennes will wipe us out too.'

The sergeant nodded. 'We best set for Stratton.'

'I don't get it,' growled one of the other men. 'Six companies pushed them Cheyennes north. Where are they?'

Forbes had been thinking the same. Over 400 cavalrymen had driven the tribe off their lands around Cheyenne Heights. This had been a spectacular disaster. The likelihood, almost certainly, would be a military and government inquiry to follow. Every officer's actions would come under scrutiny. Forbes struggled to make sense of it all. Then, tension twitching his jaw, he pondered his next move.

If he rode his troop there, what kind of logic was that? Twenty-four men, one NCO and an officer — what could his detachment do but die? No, as Jones had suggested, better to head to one of the settlements and summon help.

'We ride for Stratton,' Forbes bellowed. 'There isn't a thing any of us can do right now.'

12

A swig of whiskey and the old woman's attention to his ankle cured Tom sufficiently for him to stand. Now, as he shook his head, a look of bewilderment inched across his face.

'How did I . . . '

'I'm Walter Garvin and I hauled you in from the boardwalk,' one man cut in. He shrugged, then snorting, 'Oh, that's OK, don't thank me, Deputy. I save lawmen all the time.'

Tom proffered a smile. 'I do thank you — surely.'

The man nodded. 'If what we heard is right . . . ' He trailed off and frowned. 'Well, if Canning is dead then that makes you sheriff now.'

'Yeah,' Tom growled. 'Listen, I don't know what's happening in that saloon but it's my duty to find out. I need back-up.'

Garvin nodded. 'This is my hardware store. I've gotten a shotgun and two rifles out back.' He jabbed a hand at the two other men present in his store. 'Zeb and Stan, you can take the Winchesters; I'll use the double-barrel.'

The old woman cackled. 'They're not much to look at as a posse,' she said, 'but they'll do in a hurry.'

Tom nodded. 'How long was I out for? I mean . . . the outlaws?'

'Don't worry,' returned Garvin. 'It's only been a short time and we've got locals outside covering the saloon. If those murdering curs show their faces they'll be sorry on it.'

Tom sighed. 'Thank God for — '

The crashing open of the store's door curtailed his words. He watched aghast then as Ella hurtled into view. She stumbled, almost fell, but, after righting herself, she was on him in an instant.

'Don't do it,' she howled. 'Dear God, I'm sorry, Tom.' She dragged his face towards her own, her kisses swamped his lips. 'Pa tried to stop me but I got away.' Her eyes flashed with fear. 'Don't go and leave me. Let others die!'

He forced her away, though it pained him to do it.

'No, woman, I love you but I won't go against my duty.'

She slumped down and wrapped her arms around his legs.

'I won't let you,' she wailed. 'I'll never let — '

The old woman moved in. She gripped Ella, hauled her to her feet and stilled her blubbering with a swingeing slap.

'Hush that carry-on.' Ella reeled and sank into a chair. 'Now,' the old woman said decidedly, 'this deputy and the men will set to the saloon.' She laid a hand to Ella's hair. 'We'll wait while our menfolk make Stratton safe.'

★   ★   ★

Two Montana veterans, Calder and Swain, brought some semblance of order. Luckily, the majority of the pan men had brought weapons to the digging sites and now, the crack of gunfire sounding across the heights, the prospectors fought back.

Calder, squatting behind a large rock, cocked his Winchester and scanned the climbing approach of two knife-wielding Cheyennes.

'Jeez,' he spat. 'This doesn't look good.'

'Albert,' muttered Swain who squatted near by, 'we always said we'd blast each other if the time ever came.'

Calder, watching shocked at the advancing Cheyennes, gave a curt nod. 'Don't worry, Jim. That still stands.'

Now as they waited, their rifles to hand, the following minutes sickened them all. A mélange of noise filled their ears: gun blasts, screams and howls. The screams most of all turned their guts.

Calder succumbed at last to a sob. With that swallowed down, he slammed a finger to the trigger and the rifle bucked in his hold. When his gun's bellow faded, a Cheyenne spun into a tumbling, wailing descent. The buck settled far below, lodged between rocks, whilst Calder drew a bead on another.

'No,' Swain intoned. 'Let me do it.' He fixed to the target and felt his Winchester lurch. It roared like hell itself, flame streaking out of the muzzle as the slug went. When the Cheyenne man died, a bullet to his head spraying the slope with blood, Swain laid his rifle aside and shrugged. He watched the cadaver plunge below and he muttered a prayer.

* * *

Out on Main Street again, Tom deployed his force. He'd rallied more locals than he'd expected: eleven men in total and all of them armed. Six would set to the rear of the saloon. They'd cover the exit from the alleyways and prevent escape. Now, Tom considered those men who were left. Beside Garvin and that pair, Zeb and

Stan, there were two other middle-agers with concern in their eyes. They'd all volunteered, though, and that counted for a lot.

'We'll cover the front of the Rolling Cloud,' Tom said firmly. 'They'll be trapped and they'll have to surrender or die.'

'What about Fred Smith?' Garvin asked. 'He could be caught if shooting starts.'

'Listen,' Tom growled. 'I've a hunch Fred Smith is up to his neck in something but I've got no proof. Until I'm sure, if there's any chance of Smith being hit we will hold our fire.'

Soon, navigating that walkway, they closed on the saloon.

'Now,' hissed Tom, 'if we need to, shoot straight with some guts behind it!'

★　★　★

Lucas's eyes spoke volumes.

'Hell's sake, Cal,' he spluttered. He

and Fielding had checked the rear exit to the saloon to see armed men approaching at the run along the alleyway. They'd rapidly bolted that door and dragged boxes across to block it. 'They've gotten us trapped.'

Fielding shook his head. 'It's the Devil's choice: out front or back we're facing enough guns!'

'Shut your squawking,' Stark roared. His face contorted to a scowl but evident doubt flashed in his eyes. He looked starkly at O'Malley. 'What do you think, Irish?'

O'Malley shrugged. 'We're between a rock and a hard place,' he groaned. 'We've got to go out blasting either way.'

'This is madness,' screamed Fred Smith, still fighting to be free of Stark's hold. 'You step out there you'll all be dead.'

Stark nodded. 'Yeah,' he said sourly. 'My daddy said we'd all got a slug with our name on it.' He chuckled then and forced Smith towards the batwings.

'Except that the one that's destined for me will go through you first!'

* * *

'I've got to save him,' howled Ella, lunging for the door.

She didn't get there. The old woman, her swift movement belying her age, brought the headstrong livery widow under control. She belted Ella again and sent her reeling backwards into a shelf. A moment later, as Ella staggered down clutching her shoulder, the old woman lifted a broom.

'I'll beat you senseless with it if you keep on.'

Ella collapsed in sobs. 'You bitch,' she wailed. 'You'd stop me saving Tom.'

'Saving?' snorted the old woman, laying the broom aside. 'From what I hear, your carrying on cost one man his life. I won't let you put another in his grave.'

Ella collapsed to the floor and buried her head in her hands. When she looked up again, her eyes flooded with tears, she looked destroyed.

'I can't live without him. If anything happens I'd rather — '

'Rot,' snapped the old woman, who was now guarding the entrance. 'We women survive. It's them pigs of men what get destroyed!'

* * *

They inched on to the boardwalk to face a levelled array of five cocked guns.

'Well, lawman,' growled Stark. 'That's some arsenal you've set against us.'

'There's more besides,' spat Tom. 'We've gotten — '

'Yeah,' cut in Stark. 'There're men in the alley too.' He dragged Fred Smith to stand in front of him as a shield. 'I'd not reckon you'll want to be loosing slugs when this saloon man could die?'

Smith, his pinched features drenched in sweat, shook his head. 'Please, Stafford. This man means to kill me. I don't want to die.'

'He'll only die if you start shooting,' snarled Stark. 'Now, you and your two-bit posse, start backing off.'

Tom shook his head. 'So you're Caleb Stark?'

Stark grinned. 'And you, lawdog, are Marshal Stafford.'

Tom's eyes blazed. 'I was when I killed your kid brother.'

'Now you're deputy in this dung-hole town.' Stark laughed. 'Who'd have thought it? All these miles and years and you shove your stinking carcass up in this patch.'

'Zane had to die,' returned Tom calmly. 'I had no choice.'

Stark nodded. 'That's the way it goes, right enough. Still, Stafford, you must've known I'd want revenge.'

'Yeah,' Tom answered. 'I'd guessed you wanted me dead.'

'I tried,' returned Stark icily. 'But I just couldn't get to you.' He smirked sinisterly. 'Still, there're other ways — '

He stopped short as Tom's finger

teased at the trigger. 'What d'you mean by that? Talk damn you or so help me you die!'

'No, Stafford!' The voice of Mayor Gill sounded urgently from one of Main Street's doorways. 'An innocent man's life is at stake. Let them go, for pity's sake.'

Tom had the urge to spin round and tell the elected official what he thought of that. God alive! Let that scarfaced slayer Caleb Stark just ride off into the sunset with whatever ill-gotten gains he'd achieved from Frederick Smith? There wasn't a chance in hell. Stark was a curse on the world and he had to be wiped from it. Before he died though, he had to talk. What had the scarfaced killer just said: there were other ways for revenge? Dear Lord, had he had any part in the slaying of Lorna and Lizzie?

Garvin and the other posse men started to back away but Tom's bellowed order stilled them.

'Stand your ground,' he roared. He

fixed Stark with a searing glare. 'My wife and child,' he spat. 'So help me, Stark, if you know — '

If Stark intended to answer, Tom would never know. The mayor's clattering run along the boardwalk stilled further words. Gill, risking his own life, hurtled forward to grab Tom's arm.

'Get a grip, Sheriff,' Gill cried. 'It'll be a bloodbath on this street and that can't be risked.'

Rage rose as bile and Tom swallowed it down. His mind, numbed by what Stark had just said, still sparked with ploys. The outlaws, he decided, must have tethered their mounts at the edge of town. To achieve their means of escape Stark and his partners would have to navigate the alleyways.

'OK, we'll move off,' Tom bellowed out. 'But each posse man here keeps his gun levelled.'

They withdrew then, with careful retreated steps that made Tom's guts turn.

Stark smirked. 'They won't shoot,

like I said. We'll soon be out of here and rich as kings.'

O'Malley's pensive look said it all. Their lives rested on a knife-edge and quitting that town might not be so easy. They walked on, with slow, deliberate steps that they covered with their guns. Stark still gripped Smith tightly and shoved the saloon man out in front.

Tom, still urged back by Gill and the posse, struggled against his anger. He weighed options and felt swamped with despair. Finally, he became resolved. Whatever happened on that sun-baked street, Stark and his thug partners wouldn't reach the alleys. In that myriad of passageways, they'd achieve the upper hand. No, this affair had to conclude on Stratton's central thoroughfare.

Tom visualized the end — Stark's escape route barred and the man getting desperate. Slugs would fly, perhaps Smith and posse men would die because of it. That price, though, might have to be paid. Whatever it took,

Tom resolved, he'd ensure that the scarfaced psychopath would never rob and kill again.

A solitary, gut-turning scream sent all out of control.

Ella, with the old woman distracted and her guard lowered, had bolted for the door. Bursting on to the planks, she sighted Tom and that scream broke from her lips. She lunged for Tom. When her flailing body slammed into his, the jolt spilled the gun from his grip and it clattered to the ground.

'Goddamn it,' he roared, pushing Ella roughly away.

She screamed as she dropped, slamming down on to the walkway and making the posse men scatter.

Stark saw his chance. He brought the butt of his gun down on to Fred Smith's head. As the saloon man sank to his knees with a grunt, Stark lurched forward and grabbed a fistful of Ella's hair. He dragged her up fast, putting his gun to her temple.

'Now I know you'll back off,' Stark

yelled in triumph. 'This has got to be your bit of skirt, Stafford?'

Tom lurched forward but the hands of the posse men held him still. He flailed against their hold but he couldn't break free.

'Jeez,' he spat venomously, 'I've got to — '

'No,' Garvin barked. 'Your trying to act the hero could get Ella killed.'

An anguished howl broke along the street and Stanley Farrell jog-trotted along the dirt thoroughfare at his best speed. He'd followed events through the flung-open doorway of the livery barn, a local youth describing it all against Stanley's weakening eyesight. When Ella showed, Stanley's guts lurched. Right now, it was as if the only thing that moved on that sun-baked street was old Stanley, inching to danger at a shuffling run. All else stilled before that clapboard backdrop of summer-scorched buildings. Those armed men on the boardwalk all waited now — each of them like a static actor in some nightmarish play.

The appalling drama ran on though. Stanley, reaching the stand-off, gasped for air and shook his head. He straightened his aged body and fixed Stark with a look of pleading.

'Please, mister,' said Stanley tremulously and with his features crumpling. 'Don't hurt my little gal?'

'Grandpa,' snarled Stark. 'Do what I say and she lives.'

Stanley blinked his compliance. 'Yes sir, I'll do what it takes to keep my Ella safe.'

Tom, flooded with fury, bucked violently against the hands that held him. Writhing, spitting with anger, he tried to get his arms loose. It was to no avail though. At last, both wearied and resigned and with the promise of a gun butt across his skull if he fought on, Tom subsided.

'No, Stanley,' he ranted at the old man though. 'You can't do it. You can't help these dogs escape.'

'I've got to, Mr Stafford,' the aged liveryman muttered, 'for Ella's sake.' He nodded at Stark. 'OK, what do you want?'

Stark grinned. 'Go to Grove Street and collect our horses. You bring them here to Main Street, fast.'

Stanley nodded and spun to face the livery. 'Jack,' he yelled, 'get over here now!'

The youth reluctantly showed. He walked, trepidation set in his face along Main Street. He got to Stanley and eyed the array of guns with a fearful look.

'Mr Farrell,' the boy said hoarsely, 'my ma sure wouldn't want me involved in such doings as this.'

'Hush,' the elderly liveryman rebuked. He shoved the boy towards an alley. 'We've got horses to bring.'

They moved off and were soon out of sight down an alley. Behind them, the stand-off continued in tense silence. There, on Stratton's sun-baked thoroughfare, men straddling both sides of the law held each other at bay with drawn guns.

Time seemed to die. It meant nothing — every indeterminate second stretched into a tension-racked lifetime. Each man's eyes were filled with fear and hate but not a person among them uttered a word. Main Street was a wire-tight world where even a twitched muscle could lead to gun rage and carnage.

When the strained quiet did break, to the sound of Fred Smith's pained groan as he roused from his stupor, the saloon owner sat groggily up and set a hand to his head. That very same moment, Old Stanley and the livery boy led four horses into view.

Tom, raging with hate and despair, cursed the world as the outlaws mounted and Stark dragged Ella up on to his mustang.

O'Malley and Fielding turned first, urging their horses to the edge of town before they levelled their guns back at the posse. Then Stark and Lucas rode.

With all their mounts steadied where the street fringed the plain, Stark laughed.

'You've got to know, Stafford,' the scarfaced killer bellowed, 'that lughead in your jail didn't shoot those miners.'

'No,' railed Tom through gritted teeth, 'it was you!'

'Yeah,' Stark yelled, 'but it don't matter none. Many were to die; including your bitch here.' Stark shrugged. 'That saloon man set to pay us to kill Missy Farrell here and your sheriff.'

Tom's guts turned. Stark's cruel words rang true. Hadn't both Canning and Ella attested to Smith's festering hatred over the death of his son? Such hatred, Tom had witnessed before, makes men pay any amount of money to see their enemies slain.

'I wanted you dead,' Stark bellowed as his mount speeded on to the prairie. 'But that'll have to wait.'

Soon, as the lifted dust of their departure dissipated, the hands restraining Tom loosed their hold. He sank to his knees and his head slumped. His first grief wasn't yet quelled and now he had another one wrenching his life apart.

13

'That kind of thinking's just plain crazy,' barked Mayor Gill. He thrust a glass of whiskey across the jailhouse desk. 'Do it yourself or take a posse, the result's the same. Ella's certain to be shot.'

Tom swigged the redeye before slamming the glass down.

'But Carl, I can't just sit here hoping.' Anguish racked his face. 'I've got to do something to help Ella.'

Gill nodded understandingly. 'You will, Tom. We all will, but charging on to that prairie like a raging bull isn't going to help no one.'

Tom cursed and fumbled to build a smoke. Before long, the law office's quiet was broken by Fred Smith's plaintive tones.

'It's lies, Stafford. You've locked me up for something I didn't do. Please, you've just got to believe me.'

Fleet Duggan snorted derisively from an adjacent cell. 'Shut your bleating, Smith. If I get hold of you you'll have something to whine about.'

Tom, anger pulsing through him, got to his feet and cast his unlit smoke aside. He crossed the jailhouse at speed and grabbed keys off a hook. Soon, inside Smith's cell, he found the saloon man sitting forlornly on a bunk.

'You're set to hang,' Tom growled. He dropped a hand to the butt of his gun. 'Mind, if you don't start speaking the truth I might dispense some justice here and now.'

Smith's face paled and he shook his head.

'You won't slay me in cold blood, Deputy.' His words were firm but his face contorted with fear. 'It's all lies. I didn't set to have no one killed.'

Tom dragged out his Colt and applied the muzzle's end between Smith's eyes.

'It just takes a second,' he roared,

'and your brains will be against that wall and your corpse at my feet.'

Smith's guttural wail distracted Gill from his whiskey and he hurried across.

'Stop,' the mayor yelled. 'This isn't the way, Stafford.'

'Help me, Mayor,' howled Smith. 'This maniac don't believe me, whatever I say.'

'You're involved,' spat Tom, resisting the urge to shoot. He bedded his gun and hauled Smith to his feet. 'Just tell me,' he growled, pressing his face close, 'where are they headed?'

Smith gulped and when he spoke, his words shook. 'If I say, will it help me?'

Tom sighed. 'Hell knows. You've not got much to lose.'

Smith, sweating profusely, muttered, 'They'd gotten some crazy notion about the Cheyenne Heights. I told them to stay away.' Smith's face crumpled. 'You got to believe me, Stafford. They're all liars. I'm innocent and they've set me up.'

Tom, fighting his urge to blast Smith

where he stood, spun angrily away and stood in the corridor where Gill soon joined him. Tom slammed the cell door shut and quickly locked it.

'You'd best be speaking the truth,' he spat through the bars. 'Or I will kill you.'

He stalked into the office and retook his seat. Gill, sliding into his chair, shook his head. He watched as Tom shakily built a new smoke.

'The judge will be here in a week,' Gill observed. He took up his drink again and sipped at the whiskey. 'A trial will decide who's speaking the truth.'

Tom nodded.

Gill put his glass aside. He reached into a pocket of his jacket and produced the sheriff's star.

'Canning's at the funeral house and his wife's with him.' He put the star on the desk. 'It's yours now.'

Tom shrugged. 'It won't mean a thing if I don't get Ella safe.' His eyes described his hurt and he shaped his lips to say more when a pounding of

152

hoofbeats in Main Street stilled him.

They both lurched up and sped out to the boardwalk. There, Tom watched aghast as a troop of two dozen cavalrymen reined to a halt.

'I'm Colonel Forbes,' called one man, sliding off a horse. He strode up the walkway steps. 'You're the sheriff?'

'Yeah,' growled Gill before Tom could speak. 'He sure is, and I'm the mayor.'

Forbes nodded. 'I'd be obliged if my men and I could bed down in town tonight. We're set for reinforcements in the morning and then we'll return to the Cheyenne Heights.'

Tom's guts turned. 'Colonel,' he growled, 'have a drink in the jail and let's talk some.'

Half an hour later Forbes put aside a glass with a sigh.

'Stafford,' he said wearily, 'there're thirty mad as hell Cheyenne bucks about them hills as we speak. It's likely they've slaughtered every miner up there.'

Tom seethed with rage. 'Hell's teeth,' he spat. 'You can't just ride off.' His eyes burned. 'Goddamn it, my woman's been took there!'

Forbes shrugged. 'I'll be criticized. I take a troop up to those hills and we get slain they'll say — '

'It won't matter, will it?' Tom bellowed. 'You'll be dead and what they say don't matter a fig then!'

Forbes threw back his whiskey and gasped. He set the glass down on the desk and pinned Tom with a determined look.

'Stafford, you'd best know something.' He anchored Tom with a withering glare. 'It took a heck of a lot of soldiers to clear those heights in the first place. A lot of our men died doing it.' He looked grim. 'Fighting on the climb isn't to be recommended but, if you get a posse up, we might have the numbers to scout the foothills. Scout, mind you. No more than that.'

Mayor Gill jumped to his feet. 'I'll put

the word out and have men ready in an hour.'

'Make it two,' said Forbes, standing up himself with a weary groan. 'The horses need feed and rest.' He nodded at Tom. 'We'll do what we can.' He reached the door and frowned. 'I've served in the army thirty years and I've an unblemished record. I retire next month.' He shrugged. 'But if I'm dead why worry?'

* * *

They'd ridden hard until those dark, saw-toothed hills rose menacingly out of the distance. Now, dusk casting shadows and quelling the heat, they let their mounts pick their own pace. Ella, at the neck of the pinto and with Stark's vile breath riffling her hair, had shuddered every inch of the way.

'A few more miles,' Stark snarled, 'and we'll be knee-deep in nuggets.'

Fielding shook his head. His disquiet increased with every step they made.

Life in the army taught you many things, not least the potential of those you fought. Of all the tribes, Fielding mused now, the Cheyenne could be the Devil's own enemy. Besides, he pondered, spitting at the underfoot of sunburnt grass, that man Stark was a fool. Pan men slaved for months for an ounce of gold. They wouldn't hand it over without a struggle. Stark's unquestionable madness, though, would see any man butchered for the least gain.

Fielding threw a questioning look at O'Malley. 'Say, Pat, are you still OK with this?'

The Irishman shrugged. 'Hang it, Lee, it'll go sweet. We've dollars . . .' He broke off, his eyes narrowing as he glared at Stark. 'Hey, feller, those greenbacks you've gotten stuffed in your shirt. It needs splitting four ways.'

Stark sighed before he hauled back on his mustang's reins. Letting the leathers trail, he slid out of the saddle. When his feet hit the earth he shrugged and gave a grunt.

'Surely, boys,' he growled, dragging the canvas bag out of his clothing, 'you didn't think I'd short-change you?'

'Just split the money,' grated O'Malley, dismounting himself. 'Once I've got the dollars in my pocket I'll trust you just fine.'

Stark's look was withering but he kept quiet. He tossed the bag to ground, then dragged Ella roughly off his horse. She hit the prairie with a scream. Then, her knees buckling, she sprawled down and sobbed on the prairie.

Stark's only response was a prodded boot.

'Get up, bitch,' he snarled. 'And start counting it out.'

They all squatted down. Ella's tears stemmed as she divided the money into piles. She dragged out the task, praying that each second's delay would allow Tom to find her and end this nightmare. She shifted the bills with shaky hands, sorting them into piles worth differing amounts to confuse the outlaws.

Stark's patience eventually broke. He drew on a smoke and fixed her with a withering glare.

'You'd best hurry up and get it right, missy,' he drawled, clutching a hand to her hair and hauling her head back. 'Or I might just sell you to the miners to boost our winnings.'

When he loosed his cruel hold, Ella went back to the task with certainty in her heart. She'd survive this at any cost. Tom would come and end her hell. She threw a despairing glance across the vast grassland and recited a prayer in her mind. Then she settled on one line from the Good Book and repeated it in her head. That mantra, although unspoken, would sound across the miles like a clarion call to Tom.

'*Lord, deliver us from evil . . .* '

★ ★ ★

Silence had fallen across the hills. It was at least an hour since the last Cheyenne attack and the hot highland afternoon was steadfastly running on to evening, Calder eyed his remaining shells with a grim look.

'God alive,' he hissed, 'we've got to make each shot count.'

Swain shook his head. 'Trouble is, Albert,' he observed sourly, 'there could be more Indians than we've got bullets.'

A tense quietness settled once more; then the agonizing moments, through which each of them considered his own demise, were suddenly broken by a clatter of stones. Thrown into panic, men jerked about and shakily levelled their guns. Luckily for those who descended towards them, no rifle fired.

On the slope above, scrambling slowly downwards more armed miners had set out to reinforce their numbers.

'Jeez,' growled one man when they got there. 'Some won't leave their digging spots.'

'The stupid fools,' barked Calder angrily. 'What good is the gold if we're all scalped by nightfall?'

The other shrugged. 'You reckon that

Eli and those others are . . . ?' He trailed off, the futility of his own words dawning grimly on him.

Calder scowled as he recalled those gut-loosing wails they'd all heard earlier.

'Unless I'm mistaken,' said Calder sombrely, 'there won't be a thing alive in the shanty camp.'

Swain's face paled. 'Maybe we should go up top again and get all the men behind rifles?'

Calder nodded and gazed at the sky. The sun began to slip below the peaks.

'Look,' he gasped. 'I'd say it'll be pitch dark in a couple of hours.' He gulped. 'That could be the end of us.'

Swain spat at a rock. 'Yeah.' He sighed as they began to climb. 'It sure looks that way.'

14

A worn trail led up into the foothills. Soon, as the path became steeper and cloaked by trees, they dismounted and lashed the mounts. Near by, empty wagons congested the space beside a rustically built corral. Inside that pen six horses paced about.

'The camp can't be far,' hissed Stark. 'We'll walk from here.'

They moved on, following a route through the trees. Eventually, when the thickening canopy dulled their route, they stood a while and let their eyes adjust. In that brief pause Lucas's frayed nerves broke. A scurrying sound in the underbrush had him lunging for his gun. The flash of a rabbit's tail crossed their path.

'Damn it,' Lucas spat. 'I almost blasted the son of a bitch.'

Stark shook his head. 'Get a grip,

Lucas,' he snarled. He steadied his own lurching guts. 'This is it, boys,' he said. 'We'll rob the camp before setting up to the nugget site.' He grabbed a handful of Ella's hair and spat angrily. 'Now, what's to be done about you, missy?'

Ella screamed and tried to break free. She couldn't dislodge his hold, though, and she gasped against the pain, hating herself. She'd made hard work of the climb, sinking to her knees at any excuse. Each time, Stark had hauled her upright, spitting a curse as he did so. Now, when he loosened his hold, she collapsed with exhaustion and fought for breath.

'I've got to rest,' she gulped. 'Please — let me stop!'

Stark shook his head. 'You keep falling,' he snarled, 'and I'll make it so you'll stay down for good.'

Fielding wiped his brow with a sleeve. 'It's as hot as Hades, for sure. I'll be a sight happier when we get out of these trees.'

They moved again, Stark hauling Ella

upright and keeping a hold of her arm. Struggling on, they followed the twisting trail until the forest thinned and dim evening light broke through the canopy. Now, sighting the ramshackle shanty, they waited.

'It sure looks quiet,' growled Fielding uneasily. 'I've got to say, this place looks deserted.'

Stark nodded. The camp's stillness both disconcerted and chilled them all. Thirty or more lean-to shacks stood in utter stagnancy and quiet. Right then, in that chilling dusk, it was as if they had come upon a ghost town.

'Yeah,' Stark growled. 'It don't look right!'

'Let's go,' whined Lucas. 'We've gotten dollars enough.'

Stark stilled his partner with his levelled Colt. 'Stay your ground, mister. I said it don't look right; I didn't say we'll turn up our noses at this much gold.'

He shoved Ella forward and they inched into the camp. Soon, finding a hut door ajar, he waggled his gun at Lucas.

'Get in there and take a look.'

Lucas gasped before stepping tentatively forward. He hovered at the door, his look beseeching, but then he moved on through.

Inside, Lucas bedded his gun and started to retch. Then he lurched outside.

'Oh, God,' he howled, sinking to his knees. He fought to quell the rise of bile and clutched a hand to his mouth. When he lowered his hand again, his fingers wouldn't stay still.

'What is it?' Stark pressed with savage impatience. 'What goddamn . . .' Lucas's horror-stricken look stilled his words.

'It's bad,' Lucas gasped. 'You don't want to see it.'

Stark hesitated a moment before stepping in. When he returned, pale-faced and with his steely-eyed glare dulled, he wore a look of haggard sickness.

'I've slain enough in my time,' he

muttered, 'but that man died rough!'

O'Malley threw a panicky look at Fielding. Then he fixed Stark with a demanding glare.

'Dead, you say?'

'Butchered,' growled Stark as he thumbed back his Colt's hammer, 'and the blood still not dried.' He spat at the dirt. 'Whoever killed the son of a bitch has got . . . ' His words died and he sighed deeply. He gestured with his gun. 'This is it, boys. I'd say we're up to our necks about now.'

They all turned, terror chilling their blood. All about the shanty, Cheyenne bucks moved into view. Soon, surrounded, Stark and the others knew the end could be close.

Stark girded his nerve. He jabbed with his Colt.

'Back off, you heathen bastards,' he snarled, 'or I'll send you to whatever kind of hell waits for Indians!'

O'Malley shook his head before anchoring Stark with a despairing glare.

'We're done for,' he gasped. 'We

might blast a few but we'll suffer for it when the others get to us.'

Lucas dragged himself to his feet. 'By the look of that man in there,' he wailed, jabbing a hand at the hut, 'we'll suffer either way!'

'We're dead,' gasped Fielding, hauling out his own revolver. 'I'll say this, mind; they won't take me alive.'

Despite her own numbing despair, Ella felt a surge of triumph. 'You know what it feels like now.' Her eyes burned and she shook with hatred. 'Get to your knees and beg for mercy!'

Stark fixed her with harsh eyes.

'I don't know why you're crowing, bitch,' he snarled. 'They'll kill us straight out. It won't be half as easy for you.'

Ella, her bravado shattered, emitted an anguished howl. She sank to the ground and let the tears flow. Whilst she wept, regret coursed through her. After years of embittered loneliness, she'd found the companionship she craved. Tom Stafford, a knight in shining armour, a stranger who'd ridden off the plains to steal her heart and give her hope. It wasn't to be, though. If these outlaws didn't slay her then the Cheyennes would. Worse still, if the Indians took her she'd live out her life in wretched enslavement. Better to die, she resolved, as her tears petered out. She'd be a captive no more; her soul, God willing, would wait in heaven for the one she loved.

Up on her feet, she brushed a hand to her clothes and then stood straight. She'd face death bravely, she resolved. She watched intently, her countenance set like stone, as a solitary buck approached. When the Cheyenne man reached them, confusion flickered in Ella's eyes.

That fact that one Indian strode unarmed and unfaltering towards four drawn guns was affecting enough; what she saw when he drew close left her gasping.

This Native, a man whom Ella guessed to be in his twenties, was possessed of blond hair and the most striking blue eyes. Cheyenne he might be but once, God knew when, he'd been an American.

The blond-haired buck, standing haughtily before them, applied a finger to Stark's facial scar.

'You come here to die,' he said in faultless English. He dropped his hand and anchored Stark with a piercing look. 'But blood is nothing to you. That is said in your eyes.'

Stark sighed. 'Mister,' he answered stoutly. 'I don't deny I've killed. But I never killed a Cheyenne.' He threw his arms out wide in supplication. 'I weren't seeking trouble with you people.'

'You came to Cheyenne Heights,' answered the blond buck icily. 'In these hills any white man dies!'

'Now, just you wait a moment,' spluttered Stark, his face racked by both anger and fear. 'We came here to help you Cheyennes out.' He glanced furtively at O'Malley and Fielding. 'You tell him, boys.' When neither said a word, Stark spat a curse before pleading, 'We just wanted to make them miners leave.'

Ella, fury rising as bile, lurched forward but Stark's gripping fist held her still.

'He's lying, mister,' she screamed whilst struggling to break loose. 'Don't listen to him; don't listen to any of them. They're goddamn killers who came up here for the gold.'

Stark silenced Ella. He let go of her arm and landed a swinging fist on her face. Her head jerked violently before she slumped to the dirt. She lay there, bloodied and sobbing.

'This bitch is all gone in the head,' Stark growled. 'I've got to beat some sense into her.'

The blond buck shrugged before he bellowed out in Algonquian. Then he drilled Stark with a scornful glare.

'Some long-beards we have killed. Many more hide in the hills.' He pointed up at the higher slopes. 'I will

169

lose no more brothers to their guns. You will go; bring them here to us.'

Stark's look was pensive. 'You want us to go up there?' He shook his head. 'Hell, if we do that you'll let us walk?'

The blond buck nodded again. 'Bring the long-beards to us and we give you life.' He stepped across and helped Ella to her feet. 'This woman we keep.'

Stark grinned. 'OK. She'll make a fair enough squaw.'

The blond buck raised an arm and the Cheyennes stepped aside. Now, a way out made open to them, the outlaws took it at speed. They left the camp and set off towards the winding shale ascent to the hill's upper slopes.

They paused briefly at the edge of the camp, but then continued, their purposeful strides disguising their worries. Stark stayed resolute though. He'd been in tough situations before and had always triumphed. He'd do so again. O'Malley and Fielding sought only escape. Whatever it took, they'd live another day. Only Lucas glanced round

170

for a second time. He considered Ella and pity flooded through him. Then, shaking his head, he spun quickly and hurried after the others.

⋆ ⋆ ⋆

One of Forbes's men delivered the news.

He jabbed a hand to his left. 'A few hours ago a heck of a lot of horses went that way.' Then he shrugged and pointed to the right. 'Four horses set off on a whole different route not long since.'

Forbes nodded. 'They've all headed into the foothills?'

'Yes, sir,' said the trooper. 'It sure looks that way.'

Forbes frowned. 'It's clear enough, I reckon.' He fixed Tom with a knowing glare. 'Those Cheyennes got into the Heights way ahead of the outlaws and your woman. Luckily for them, they've off-saddled at different parts of the hills.'

'Come on, then,' growled Tom, desperation straining his face. 'We'll ride fast and — '

'Stay it, Stafford,' Forbes barked. 'We do it under my orders.' He shook his head. 'We deal with the Cheyennnes. Only after that do we go looking for your woman.'

Tom's eyes flashed. He jerked on the reins to bring his horse about but found the way blocked by armed troopers. He spun in the saddle and fixed Forbes with a furious look.

'You're a son of a bitch, Colonel,' he snarled. 'If anything happens to Ella I'll — '

'You'll get us all killed if you don't do as I say,' returned Forbes forcefully. 'I can't risk you charging half-cocked into those hills whilst those Cheyenne bucks are on the loose.'

'Goddamn it,' Tom spat. 'What if those bucks — '

'Enough,' Forbes barked. 'I'm held here arguing with you when I could be rounding up those Cheyenne renegades and making sure your woman's safe.'

Tom scowled but he swallowed back his words.

'Now,' gritted Forbes, 'I want your word you'll obey instructions and not try and do anything stupid.' He eyed Tom intently. 'If I have to, I'll relieve you of your gun and make sure you can't act crazy.'

Tom shrugged and fixed the posse men with a pleading look.

Garvin shook his head. 'I'd reckon it'd be best to stay with these soldier boys. We're talking Indians here.'

Tom, seething but resigned, fixed Colonel Forbes with a baleful look. 'What choice have I got?'

'None,' retorted Forbes with a curt nod. 'Now, we ride!'

★　★　★

'One more step,' a voice bellowed, 'and we'll blast you to hell.'

Calder ducked as a slug whipped close by his head. He growled a curse and yelled angrily, 'Don't shoot, for Christ's sake. It's us!'

He came to the top of the trail and in to the mining site with a sigh of relief. The ascent was strenuous at the best of times. On a day like this, with nerves frayed, it fatigued a man beyond endurance. They'd struggled up hundreds of feet, with shale becoming dislodged underfoot and providing a clattering warning of their approach.

'You fools,' Calder barked as he emerged on to the plateau to face an array of aimed guns. 'You've got to save bullets.'

In no time, all of the miners bunched close. Calder told them the truth.

'It's Cheyennes,' he growled. 'Maybe hundreds of them.' He blew out his cheeks. 'I'd say those in the camp are dead.'

'Oh no,' cried out a tall man. 'Eli's gone?'

Calder nodded. 'Beside Eli there were four others in the shanty. They'll all be corpses.'

A combined groan escaped the massed miners' lips.

'What now?' gasped a man called Frome. 'We can't last against that number!'

Calder nodded. 'That's a fact. I'm about out of slugs as it is.' He lifted his rifle and glanced sharply at Swain. 'I'll blast Cheyennes until my last bullet. Then, well . . . we do each other!'

Frome's eyes flashed anger. 'Damn army,' he cursed. 'Hell's teeth — we're to be scalped and not a bluebelly in sight.'

Calder sighed. 'Yeah, but squawking won't change a fig.' He reached for a cartridge. 'We've got to fathom some way out.'

*　*　*

Leaving two troopers behind to guard the horses, Forbes led his combined force on foot. He set a cautious pace, at the same time holding Tom Stafford on a tight rein.

175

'You stay close, Deputy,' he growled. 'Where I can see and get a hand to you if needed.'

Tom's spat curse brought a chuckle from one the soldiers.

'You're in this man's army now, Mr Deputy Sheriff. You do as you're told and that's all there is to be said of it.'

A curse swelled at Tom's lips but he left it unsaid. Just then, as they emerged through underbrush, they sighted tethered ponies.

A trooper approached and applied a hand to one of the ponies.

'These have been ridden hard. Most are fit for little now.'

Forbes nodded. 'OK,' he replied. 'We'll search on.' He cast a warning glare at Tom. 'We stay together and no goddamn talking.'

15

That gun blast had halted their climb. It had thundered out from the peaks above, making them all reach for their guns. Now, as the rifle's roar faded, Stark glanced around. He saw the corpse then — just to their left and lodged between rocks. He pointed a finger and they all looked.

The cadaver showed its recent wounds. Blood coated the dead buck's limbs whilst a slug had blown away most of his face.

'This isn't good,' spat Stark, shaking his head. 'It seems like those miner boys can shoot a bit.'

'Yeah,' growled Lucas, 'and we could be next.'

He scanned the ascent above. The trail just kept getting steeper, a snaking shale route between the jagged contours of the hills. Somewhere up there, perhaps hidden behind any one of the towering stone mounds they had to pass, a pan man with a rifle might lay in wait.

'No wonder those Cheyenne didn't fancy it,' Fielding growled, shaking his head. 'I heard the Fourth lost enough bodies driving the Cheyennes out of here.'

'Now they're back.' O'Malley spat and wiped his face with a sleeve. 'And unless we get them miners down we'll be dead too.'

Lucas's own face crumpled. 'What chance do we have?' he wailed as he spun about. He didn't go anywhere, though. Stark gripped his partner's coat and held him still.

'Sure, it's a tough choice, right enough. Still, I'd rather face those pan men than those goddamn bucks.'

'OK, mister,' snarled O'Malley. 'What do you reckon? I'll be damned if some skittish miner's sending me to hell.'

'Stay it,' barked Stark. 'They won't shoot at us.' He shrugged. 'I'd reckon to warn them we're on the way.' He raised his Colt and sent two slugs skyward. When the shots' echoes faded he yelled loudly, 'You hear me, miner boys? We're coming up, so stay your fingers at the trigger.'

Soon, as quiet settled over the hills again, they struggled on. Whenever Lucas faltered — for fear was beseeching him still — Stark spurred his partner with venomous threats.

At last, exhausted but thankful, they neared the summit of the trail. They squatted there awhile, gasping for breath. When they'd recovered, Stark checked his gun.

'You men up top,' he bellowed. 'You hear me calling?'

'We hear,' a voice cried in reply. 'Who are you?'

'We're your way out,' yelled Stark. 'We've done us a deal with them Cheyennes. You men hold your fire and we'll come up there and talk about it.'

'OK, but bed your guns. We'll have you covered.'

When Stark and the others finally crested the ascent, miners showed like ants spilling from a prodded nest.

Calder stepped forward, shaking his head. 'I've got to tell you boys, it's a miracle and no mistake.'

Stark eased back his hat brim. 'Yes, sir,' he said, 'we're your lucky day and that's for sure.'

Calder took in the other's scarred jaw with an unsettled feeling. This quartet, the veteran pan man pondered, had the smack of trouble about them.

'I don't get it,' Calder voiced his disquiet. 'Those Cheyennes were after our blood. Now you four just walk right through them.' His looked darkened. 'What's going on?'

Stark shrugged. 'How do I know? We were going past these hills when we heard the guns.' His eyes flickered nervously. 'Call it lucky, but those Indians welcomed us with open arms. It seems they just want to do a deal.'

Swain removed his hat and wiped his brow with a sleeve.

'It don't matter squat why,' he drawled. 'I don't want to be up here when dark sets in. If the Cheyennes let us leave that'll do for me.'

Grunts of agreement sounded from the other miners.

'One of those heathens speaks our lingo,' Stark added. 'He's said it clear: you'll hand over nuggets and lay down your guns. After that, you can go.'

Calder quelled the grumbled dissent. He harangued the pan men, told them not to be foolhardy and put gain over their own lives. There'd be other strikes, he assured them; they'd live to pan elsewhere. Soon the miners, seeing the sense in Calder's words, began to turn out their pockets.

'That's right, boys,' crowed Stark. He bedded his gun and slid off his hat as a receptacle for the nuggets. That hat quickly filled. When it bulged with gleaming nuggets, Stark's eyes shone just as brightly.

'Beautiful,' he enthused, unable to take his gaze off the gleaming metal.

'You can see why those Indians want it back.'

'Say, mister,' said Calder after a moment. 'What now?'

His wish for wealth fulfilled, Stark scanned their fear-etched faces with an icy glare.

'I said it plain so you sons of bitches would understand,' he growled. 'All guns to be laid down and gold handed over.'

Soon, their rifles piled at Stark's feet, the miners stepped back and exchanged bemused looks.

Stark shook his head. He clutched the nugget-filled hat in one hand and dragged his gun up with the other. When he spoke, he spat the words through gritted teeth.

'Is this *all* the gold?'

The silence that ensued — fraught moments in which men regarded each other with terrified eyes — soon broke.

'Hell, I'll say it,' one miner gasped. He jabbed an accusing finger. 'Larry Green's got a couple of stones hidden in his boot.'

Men parted and Stark passed his nugget-weighted hat to Lucas. A moment later, he was face to face with Larry Green.

'That right, mister? You've been holding out on me?'

Green gulped. 'It's a goddamn lie. I handed my bits in.'

Stark scratched at his nose with the end of his Colt's muzzle.

'I've got this itch,' he drawled. 'I just can't shift it.'

Green looked perplexed. 'Look, feller, I don't get it.'

'You'll get it all right,' spat Stark, hauling up his gun, 'right to the gates of hell!'

Through flame and smoke, a slug left Stark's Colt and ripped into Green's guts. The man dropped fast, his hands clutching pathetically at a gaping wound as he crashed on to his back and lay in eternal stillness. Stark stepped up and dragged off Green's boots. He found the concealed nuggets and fixed an ominous glare on the other miners.

'Fellers,' he rasped, 'don't hide gold from me, or by God every son of a bitch among you will die!'

★　★　★

'Damn it, Stafford,' spat Forbes. 'Are you crazy?'

Tom, running when that last gun blast roared, now lay prostrate, restrained by several men. They'd brought him crashing to earth and taken possession of his Colt. He struggled, trying to dislodge the hands that held him down, but soon he succumbed.

'Enough,' Forbes snarled. 'Get him on his feet.'

As he was dragged upright Tom muttered a curse.

'I've got to get to Ella,' he gasped. 'Those shots might — '

'If they have,' snapped Forbes, 'there's nothing you can do about it.' The colonel shook his head. 'Do you reckon you're so special? You're one man. You planning on confronting four outlaws, a heck of a lot of Cheyenne — *and* all those miners to boot?'

Tom scowled, swallowing back his rage.

'I'll try,' he snarled. 'I'll be out there doing something instead of skulking in these trees like a damn ... ' He stopped himself from saying it before his head slumped. When he looked up again, he looked bereft. 'I don't want her to die, Forbes,' he spluttered. He stifled a sob. 'I need her!'

Forbes's tone altered. 'It's OK, Stafford,' he said softly. 'We'll get to your woman, I promise.'

Tom nodded and the hands holding him lifted away. Rubbing the pain in his back, Tom fixed Forbes with a harsh look.

'What about my gun?'

'I'm not sure,' said Forbes evenly, 'whether I can trust you.'

'This is crazy,' Tom spat then. 'I'm a deputy sheriff and I've got the jurisdiction.'

'Not here,' Forbes retorted icily. 'Not

now. I'm in charge. This is army business and it'll get dealt with how I say.' He thrust out a hand and one of the troopers passed over Tom's Colt. 'Now,' growled Forbes, 'I'll give you this back on trust.'

Tom sucked in air, then he nodded.

'Right,' said Forbes, shoving the Colt into Tom's hand. 'We'll move forward slow and quiet.'

They pushed on, Tom cursing through gritted teeth as the pace slowed yet more. They advanced now — literally by inches — across the vast span of that forest.

Go to hell, Tom muttered in his mind. *While you creep in here, I'll be out in the hills doing what I do best.* Then he ran, plunging through the underbrush like a man possessed.

When he eventually came to a halt, he knelt and stared blandly at his scratched and bloodied hands. He'd hurtled through thorn shrubs like they didn't exist. All the way, Forbes's anguished calls had followed.

'For goodness' sake, Stafford, this is

madness. Don't do it, man! You can't deal with this alone.'

Tom ran on again, a tight grip on his gun and the vengeance of hell coursing through his veins.

16

His words came edged with tenderness. 'Do not fear. You will not be hurt, this I swear.'

Ella shuddered and stifled a sob of relief. She let her lips relax to a smile and her eyes studied him intently.

'Your name?' she muttered. 'I'd like to know.'

'Snow Wolf,' he said. He sighed then. 'My white name was Matthew . . . Matthew Standish.' His face clouded. 'For so long I did not speak it.'

'Snow Wolf,' she muttered. 'I know what it's like to be taken. To have your destiny denied you.' When he didn't answer she wiped her eyes. 'My destiny was to marry Tom Stafford and have the life I always wanted. Now you'll . . . '

'The scarface,' he murmured. 'And the men that ride with him — it is their guns that call out.'

Ella nodded. 'They're animals.' She stood silent then, her eyes lowered. When she looked up again, her face showed her terror. 'You'll keep me here?' she gasped. 'Then the scarfaced man and those dogs with him will kill me.'

'Why do you not believe?' he asked. He gestured a hand at the other Cheyenne bucks. 'They seek blood for what has happened here, but not yours.'

She shuddered at that. She blanked the notion of death from her mind, tried to keep this man, her one chance of survival, talking. 'Matthew,' she pressed. 'What of your first family?'

He clearly pondered the matter with some intensity, his brow furrowing and his eyes bright. At length he muttered, 'All dead. Six white men came to our farm and killed all: Mother, Father, sister, two brothers.'

'Dear God,' she exclaimed. 'But there must be others? What of your grandparents; your aunts and uncles?'

He tilted his head to one side and his

eyes narrowed. 'Grandparents dead,' he said quietly. 'My aunt and uncle are still in Missouri, I think. They are Albert and Mary Standish.'

'Missouri?' Ella exclaimed. She stretched a hand out and clutched his. 'Matthew, my man's from that state. If anyone can find your family Tom Stafford will.'

He frowned. 'Tom Stafford?'

'The man who'll come for me,' she said decisively. 'He'll deliver me out of this nightmare. He'll find your folks.'

Snow Wolf smiled. 'My Cheyenne father is with the Spirits. I never spoke of my white life. I remembered all. Always I did.'

'And now,' she said intensely. 'What do you want?'

'What I know will not happen. The Cheyenne way is over. This that we do now, it is of no account. Many scores of bluebellies will come. We will all die.'

'No,' she wailed, lurching to her feet and gripping his hand. 'I'll make them see. I'll make them let *you* survive.'

'But the Cheyenne,' he sighed, '*they*

will not survive.'

'I can't stop the will of a government,' she said unhappily. 'No, that no one can do, much as we might want to.'

'Too many white men and not enough land,' said Snow Wolf pensively. 'That is what my Cheyenne father said.'

Ella nodded. 'That's about the whole of it.'

Snow Wolf pointed a finger at an older Cheyenne who was squatting near by. 'Our Medicine Father Two Moons says our ancestors cry for blood. This we must obey.'

'You can prevent this slaughter!' she cried. 'You can persuade these Cheyennes to forgive.'

'If your father's bones were dug up and scattered,' returned Snow Wolf, 'would you?'

* * *

'It don't do to be brave,' growled O'Malley at the defiant miners. 'You'll just be a corpse with guts.'

191

The pan men, refusing to be cowed, held their ground.

'You've got our guns and gold,' growled Calder. 'And now that scarfaced bastard's murdered Larry Green. We're not listening to anything you say.'

'You *will* listen, mister,' spat Stark. 'Those Cheyenne will use your scalps as bed stuffing and that's the best of it. Hell, they've gotten them a torture, I hear — they'll tie you to your own wagon wheels and roast you over coals. How's that sound to you?'

Calder shook his head. 'They'll kill us, right enough. Damn it, they'll kill you too.'

O'Malley reacted to that. He fixed Stark with an accusing look. 'You minded how *we're* getting out of this mess?'

Stark's face wore a demented expression. He jabbed a hand at Lucas, who still clutched the hat stuffed with gold nuggets.

'I done it,' he roared. 'I got me the fortune. Down Mexico I'm a right rich man.'

'*You're* a rich man?' Fielding cried out. 'Hell, we've got quarter shares in all that!'

Stark's eyes blazed but he tamed his temper.

'Err . . . yeah, sure you have, boys.' His eyes flickered furtively and his tongue licked at his upper lip. 'First, mind, we've to get these pan men down to the Cheyennes.'

The miners bristled but Stark stilled their dissent.

'There's a heck of a lot of you,' he snarled. 'But we've got slugs enough. Do any of you long-beards want to give it a go?'

None of the miners moved. Each treasured his own life above collective stupidity.

'Right then,' shouted Stark, waggling his Colt. 'Get your stinking carcasses down this hill. Get down to them Indians and I'll see you all to hell!'

17

Fielding and Lucas went down first. Afterwards, the miners descended in a ragged, unwilling line. When the last of the pan men had left the plateau, Stark stuffed nuggets into his pockets and shook his head.

'I suppose you'll squawk for a share of this gold?' he snarled, casting a withering glare at O'Malley.

'No,' growled the Irishman sourly. 'I don't want anything else off you.' He sighed. 'When this is done, if we live, Lee and me will ride our own way.'

He set off down the trail and left Stark chuckling behind.

'Ah, come on, Irish,' the scarfaced killer urged. 'You've got to admit, this partnership's been as exciting as hell.'

★　★　★

Tom squatted in mulch and gasped for air. How long he'd been running or in which direction he wasn't sure. He'd just plunged onward, ignoring Forbes's plaintive wails. When they'd faded out, Tom let his pace slacken. Now his lungs and legs were aching; he needed rest.

As he recovered, he mused on what he'd done. God alive, Forbes's appeals to his reason had been well-judged: this *was* crazy. What could one man achieve against the numbers *he* might face: Cheyennes, outlaws, potentially violent pan men? Even so, Tom quickly decided that he'd push on alone. After all, he'd always acted thus. He'd been beholden, through twenty years, to none but the honour of his badge and those victims who'd suffered. This victim was different though. He searched for her, not for money or duty . . . but for love!

Tom struggled to his feet and crashed through a wall of whipping foliage. With more thorns tearing at his flesh, he cursed down the pain until he reached a clearing. Here, beside a collection of wagons and a roughly constructed corral, four saddled horses stamped against their lashed leathers.

Tom stepped close and he instantly recognized Stark's mustang. He felt a surge of elation, tempered by worry. Calming his excitement, he gripped his gun tightly and followed a foot-worn trail. The time of reckoning was near.

★　★　★

Huddled together at the foot of the descent, the miners' grumbling resistance grew. Fielding tried to quell it by jabbing his Colt and issuing threats of death. It didn't work — the pan men grew more hostile by the minute and seemed ready to risk a slug to get back what they'd lost.

'You robbing, murdering curs,' spat Cain. 'We break our backs for months to have you sons of bitches take our gold?'

Fielding scanned his gaze upward and noted the slow approach of O'Malley and Stark. They progressed down that snaking trail at a snail's pace. Cursing, Fielding stepped away and beckoned Lucas to follow. With room enough to shoot, Fielding waggled his gun.

'Now, boys, just wait till the others get here and we'll discuss this some more.'

The time that passed before Stark and O'Malley showed was fraught.

'What's this,' growled Stark, quickly weighing up the dissension. 'Don't be getting any ideas.'

'Go to hell,' snapped Swain. 'You think we'll — '

A sickening howl curtailed his fit of temper.

'Jeez,' cried one of the other pan men. He gestured with a trembling hand towards the shanty camp. 'Just look, will you?'

As all heads turned, they observed the menacing approach of the Cheyennes. Those bucks, knives to hand, moved steadily out of the shanty camp towards them.

Calder spun and met Stark's gaze with panicked eyes. 'No way, mister,' he spat. 'Those heathens will butcher us.'

Stark smirked. 'Sure they will.' He jabbed his Colt at Calder's head. 'And you'll be the first to die.'

Dissension swelled now to a fever pitch. Some of the pan men refused to move, dropping to the ground and pleading plaintively for mercy. Others, like Calder and Swain, stayed upright, venting curses.

'You stinking dogs,' bellowed Calder. 'Shoot me dead where I stand, but I'll not walk to a Cheyenne knife.'

Stark moved quickly. He jumped across and slammed his gun butt to Calder's temple. When the miner fell with a soft groan, Swain got to his partner's side and tried to rouse him.

As the noise of the fear-roused miners drifted into the camp, Snow Wolf nodded at Ella.

'Stay,' he said firmly. 'And do not look at what happens.'

Ella gasped, watching appalled as

Snow Wolf drew a dagger from his belt. A massacre would occur, and though she could blind herself to its bloody horror by shutting her eyes, she'd hear the pitiful cries of death sure enough.

'But surely,' she wailed at Snow Wolf. 'You won't . . . ?'

He nodded. 'They must die.'

He moved off to join his Cheyenne brethren.

Despite her resurgent terror, Ella cried out loudly, 'You bastard, Matthew Standish. How dare you; how dare you murder those poor men. Yes, they've done wrong, but just let them go and they won't come back. God alive, give it up? This is all pointless.' She burst into tears and covered her face with her hands.

Thus she stood, weeping in that hideous place, until she felt a hand tugging at her arm. She slowly lowered her hands and breathed in deeply.

'Snow Wolf,' she said. 'I just . . . '

But it wasn't Snow Wolf. Another Cheyenne stood there, his knife raised and his hand ready to plunge the blade tip into her neck. A scream gathered at her throat and her eyes clamped shut.

* * *

They gathered at the corral and Forbes sighed. He mused, with admiration, upon one of his trooper's tracking skills. With a raised hand the cavalryman indicated a noticeable pathway.

'Straight ahead, sir. We're not far behind the bastard.'

'Stay that talk, soldier,' Forbes admonished. 'Mr Stafford's nothing if he isn't brave.' The colonel shrugged. 'Mind, any of you get ideas from this, then think again. I'll have you before a firing squad if you ever disobey an order of mine.'

The tracker nodded and shaped his lips to speak. He ran though, as they all did then, towards the most awful screams!

* * *

Tom, obscured behind scrub, witnessed it all. He'd followed each sickening development and every word. His guts turned as he listened to Ella's unconditional kindness to the English-speaking buck. Desire swamped him and he ached to hold her close. Until the time was right, though, he needed to stay hidden. He saw the Cheyenne bucks rise and leave the camp; he listened, transfixed, to the chorused howl of fear and dissent that rose from the miners huddled outside the shanty.

Still he held there, fighting his impulse to charge until he couldn't wait any more.

He moved at the very point that a knife blade scythed toward Ella's throat.

Tom fired as he ran. Crashing up out of the shrub, he swung the Colt fast and sent the Cheyenne who was assailing Ella spinning off his feet. A second later the buck crashed to earth with dead, flailing hands and a gaping wound in his head.

Cheyenne bucks howled out in shock and anger. In no time, two natives raced toward Tom with vengeful death in their cries, and both with a fist aloft, scalping knives poised.

Tom, dropping quickly to one knee, sent slugs through a blazing sheet of flame. When the firing subsided, cordite choking the air, he watched with satisfaction as both bucks fell.

Up on his feet again Tom froze in shock. Though he'd just slain three Cheyenne bucks he'd set in motion unstoppable chaos amongst that huddle of miners who were just outside the camp. They scattered in all directions, a wailing unison filling the foothill's air.

'No more,' bellowed that English-speaking buck. 'Enough brothers have died.'

Tom nodded. 'The one who aimed a knife at my woman surely did.' He plunged forward with his guts lurching. Ella was running — not towards Tom and salvation. No, sheer terror prevented that. Demented by fear, she just knew she had to get away. A moment later she slammed into the outstretched arms of Caleb Stark, to her sickening horror and his utter delight.

As Stark gripped Ella tightly, Fielding and O'Malley swung their guns and dispatched multiple shots. With their gun blasts rending the air, Stark closed his hold about Ella and breathed nauseatingly in her ear.

'I knew you'd come back to me, bitch.' He dragged her violently by the hair. 'Now, I've got the top hand again!'

18

While slugs were shredding the air Tom hit the ground and rolled into the space between two shacks. He got back to his feet quickly, reloading his Colt before craning his neck to sight his target.

Stark hadn't moved. The outlaw held his station on the slope just beyond the shanty, his fist still gripping Ella's hair. A second later he dragged her upright and positioned her sob-racked body in front of him.

Tom also saw Stark's three accomplices begin to edge back towards the trail, each of them scanning the shanty whilst keeping their guns levelled.

'Don't be a fool, lawman,' Stark bellowed. 'You start towards me again, so help me I'll kill your bitch in a second.'

Tom tensed but he stayed hidden.

'Stark, if you lay another finger on Ella I'll — '

'You'll do nothing,' Stark cut in. He laughed raucously. 'Me and the boys will be getting out of these hills and this missy will be our insurance.'

Tom swallowed down a curse before he snarled, 'Say, Stark, who are your boys, anyhow? Hell, I'm sure interested to know.'

'They go by the names of O'Malley, Fielding and Lucas Cole,' snarled Stark.

Then O'Malley spun on Stark and his invective came layered with hate. 'Goddamn it, you've put our necks in a noose.'

'Yeah,' Fielding barked. 'You're a state-sized scum, Stark and I don't reckon — '

His words ended the same moment as his life. Stark, swinging his gun, dispatched a slug that slammed into Fielding's chest. He fell fast, crashing to earth, where he lay motionless and silent.

O'Malley's shock and revulsion showed. His face crumpled and he surveyed the cadaver of his partner with distress in his eyes. Soon, though, he wore a look of vengeance.

'You bastard,' he howled, dragging up his gun. 'You'll — '

The bellow of Stark's gun stilled his words and sent O'Malley hurtling away into the shadows. Stark shook his head and turned to Lucas with a determined look.

'Hey, partner — we'll get up to that mining site and find us another way out of here.'

Lucas shrugged. 'Sure, Cal,' he muttered sombrely, 'whatever you say!'

* * *

Tom inched forward but then stopped as he felt the press of cold metal at his head. When he risked a turn, he looked down the barrel of a rifle.

'Another step, Stafford,' growled a soldier, 'and my orders are to take your goddamn head off.'

Colonel Forbes appeared then, hurrying into the shack camp with the rest of his troop and the Stratton posse men.

'Jeez,' spat the cavalry officer, gazing upon slain Cheyennes and the still kneeling and supplicant surviving bucks. He fixed Tom with a demanding look. 'I take it this is your doing?'

Tom nodded. 'I killed three and the rest surrendered.'

Forbes's countenance changed to one of admiration for Tom.

'God alive — you've captured all the renegades single-handed.'

Tom gave a curse and gestured with a hand up at the ascending trail. There, steadily moving up and illumined by a now emerging moon, three figures worked their way towards the summit.

'Deal with these Indians,' Tom spat. 'I need to go after Ella. Stark killed one of his gang, but another got away and is in these foothills with the miners.'

The posse men, who had been

standing together in a group, stepped forward.

'With those Indians caught,' opined Garvin, 'it means this is a straight hunt for murderers. We'll be alongside you, Stafford.'

Tom nodded and fixed Forbes with a determined glare. 'Colonel,' he said. 'I reckon you could — '

'Stay it,' snapped Forbes. 'Get after your woman and those scumdogs who've taken her. We'll clean up things down here.'

As Tom and the posse left the shanty, Forbes appraised the blue-eyed buck he'd encountered on the plains.

'I should shoot you all here and now,' he said coolly. 'That way I'll know you'll all stay put.'

Snow Wolf rose to his feet. His eyes expressed a steely resolve.

'My brothers will go to your reservation,' he said stoutly. 'I'll . . . ' he trailed off and gulped. When he spoke again his words were infused with some deep emotion. 'I will go to

208

my family in Missouri.'

Forbes removed his hat and brushed a sleeve to his brow. He mopped sweat and considered the blond-haired buck with a resolved nod. 'OK, mister. So be it!'

Snow Wolf moved away but Forbes caught hold of his arm.

'Say, what *has* happened up here?'

Snow Wolf told him. Forbes considered what he heard with a look of bemusement.

'So you and these surviving bucks didn't kill anyone?'

'No,' said Snow Wolf icily. 'We tried, but we did not.'

'And those three men who came here with the scarface Stark?' pressed Forbes. 'Do you remember their names?'

'No,' returned Snow Wolf, 'but I will know their faces again.'

Forbes nodded. 'I take it you know these hills inside out?'

'Yes.' Snow Wolf smiled. 'I am . . . Matthew Standish.'

Forbes turned and spat at the dirt. Then he gestured at one of his men.

'Williams, take six men and go with this buck. He'll act as scout and he'll be able to identify this missing outlaw.'

Moments later, as Matthew Standish and the troopers began to move away, one of the other soldiers addressed Forbes.

'Begging your pardon, sir, but letting that buck loose to lead the men like that . . . ? You think that's so wise?'

Forbes sighed. 'I didn't make colonel by playing it safe,' he shook his head, 'no matter what that hothead Stafford thinks.'

* * *

Concealed in underbrush, Calder rubbed a hand to his head.

'Goddamn son of a bitch,' he growled. 'He's given me a headache and no mistake.

'You're alive,' Swain pointed out,

210

tapping his partner's shoulders. 'That's all that matters.'

'Yeah,' grunted Calder, looking at the third man sharing their hiding-place. 'Say, Barnes,' he said sourly, 'I meant to ask you — up there at the mining site when that scarfaced crazy man asked if we'd handed over all the gold . . . ' Calder shrugged, 'how'd the hell did you know Green had got nuggets in his boot?'

'I didn't,' returned Barnes matter of factly. 'Green owed me money for nigh on fifteen years. He wouldn't pay it back.'

Swain loosed his own boot and gave a sigh. 'It's a good job you didn't say my name. Hell, I've got enough nuggets hidden.'

'Yeah?' Barnes said. 'Me too.'

In no time the three miners clutched a decent return of gold.

'I'd guess each man up there didn't hand over what he'd mined,' drawled Barnes. 'Much as I hated Green, I didn't want the man dead.'

A sudden explosive oath close by heralded a man crashing through the tangled brushwood. An instant later, O'Malley emerged, his Colt raised.

'I heard every word, boys,' the Irishman drawled. 'Now, hand over that gold.'

Swain shook his head. 'Jeez,' he spat. 'You've robbed us twice in one night. God's teeth, where's justice?'

'Oh, you'll get justice,' growled O'Malley. He took hold of the proffered nuggets and shoved them into the pockets of his pants. He chuckled. 'You'll get slug justice.'

Moments later, as gunsmoke dissipated and the roar of his Colt quieted, O'Malley moved fast. He took off his Stetson and duster, and replaced them with the floppy hat and ripped jacket of one of the slain miners. The dead man lay in a pool of blood, with startled, wide-open eyes.

O'Malley hurled his Colt into the distance, took up a rifle and stepped out of the underbrush.

'Nice doing business with you boys,' he said cheerily as he walked away. He strode nonchalantly across the now moon-kissed foothills, whistling a cheery tune.

19

Tom, cursing loudly as those gun blasts bellowed, set the others on edge.

'Pull yourself together, Deputy,' growled one of the posse men. 'Those shots sounded below us. I'd say it's likely them soldiers, shooting the Cheyennes.'

Tom nodded and scanned the climb ahead. The trail — its snaking ascent difficult now but likely to get harder as they neared the mining site — took its toll. He thought of Ella and he fought against despair and rage. How could she manage such terrain? What terror must she be suffering? His thoughts settled on Stark and he felt fury rise as bile. That scarface maniac, Tom pledged right then, would pay for what he'd put Ella through. He'd also reveal, no matter what it took, his involvement in the deaths of Tom's wife and child.

Reality jolted Tom then. Unless he captured Stark alive, he'd not get the answers he craved. What *did* that scarface maniac know about Lorna and Lizzie's deaths?

They pushed on at the best pace they could manage. When they rested, sitting on rocks beside the trail, Tom glanced skyward. He searched for his stars and sighed as he saw them. With night now set in they shone bright — like vibrant reminders.

★   ★   ★

'Now,' a voice growled out of the dark, 'hands up, mister.'

O'Malley stopped and feigned a look of surprise. He grinned as several soldiers approached with carbines levelled.

'Why, I'm right glad to see you boys,' he cried out. 'I thought I was done for.'

Williams frowned. 'Those shots we heard — what's happened?'

O'Malley shook his head and set his

215

countenance to an expression of sadness. 'One of those robbers blasted three of my partners.' He reached into a pocket and produced a couple of nuggets. 'I got lucky and got away with my finds.'

Williams lowered his gun and gave a sigh. 'Jeez,' he growled. 'These outlaws are going to suffer for this.'

O'Malley nodded. 'They're unstable bastards right enough.'

Williams jabbed a hand in the direction of the shanty. 'We've got to hunt down this maniac,' he said firmly. 'You'd best make your own way down to the camp.'

'But ... those Indians?' returned O'Malley, in a voice made tremulous. 'What if ... ?'

'Don't worry,' Williams told him. 'They're under guard with the rest of our troop.'

O'Malley doffed the floppy hat and began to step away. He halted though as that blond-haired, blue-eyed Cheyenne emerged out of the shadows. A moment later, panic stricken, O'Malley levelled the rifle and fired. That sent a slug erupting through flame that ripped into Matthew's shoulder and sent him crashing to earth with an agonized howl.

'Jeez,' bellowed Williams, spinning about and sighting O'Malley sprinting into the distance. The soldier didn't hesitate. He dropped to one knee and sent a bullet that tore into O'Malley's right calf. Brought slamming to earth, O'Malley writhed in pain before trying to get to his feet. He soon gave up, watching forlornly as Williams and the other troopers reached him.

'God alive,' growled Williams. 'I'm sorry, feller.' He shook his head. 'I should have told you one of those Cheyenne bucks was acting as our guide. He must've scared you silly.'

O'Malley, biting down the burning hurt in his leg, groaned through gritted teeth, 'Why the hell did you blast me?'

'I had to bring you down,' Williams replied. 'If you'd run into the shanty after all this gunfire you'd have skittered the troopers and . . . ' He shrugged. 'You're winged but still alive.'

O'Malley did his best to grin. 'I'd be obliged if — '

His words choked off as Matthew, supported by a soldier, shuffled into view.

'He is the one,' gasped Matthew weakly. He pointed at O'Malley. 'He came to these hills with the scarfaced one.'

Williams pushed up his hat brim and fixed O'Malley with a savage look.

'Damn it,' he spat. 'Now I wish I'd blasted you in the back.'

O'Malley's guts turned. Fear welled as bile and he couldn't stop the shudder that racked his body.

'Now, boys,' he implored. 'You can't believe no scumdog Indian over a — '

'Shut up,' snapped Williams. He raised his own gun and sent two shots skyward. As his rifle's roar subsided, Williams yelled, 'You pan men out there — it's safe to show yourselves. This is

Private Williams of the US Cavalry shouting.'

Gradually, agonizingly slowly at first but then in rapid succession, people emerged. Now, as all the miners huddled about the soldiers, Williams pointed at O'Malley.

'Can any of you pan men vouch for this feller?'

One man stepped forward and nodded grimly.

'He's one of the robbers.' He gestured at the clothes O'Malley wore. 'I take it that hat and stuff is from the miner you blasted?'

'Yeah,' growled another. He glanced about with a sombre look. 'Calder and Swain aren't here. Neither is Barnes.'

'Three shots we heard,' observed Williams. 'Now, three miners are missing.' He fixed O'Malley with a piercing glare. 'Where are their bodies?'

Ten minutes later, the corpses located, O'Malley's face grew pale and he considered Williams with fearful eyes.

'I'd be obliged for a swift finish, soldier boy.'

Williams shook his head. 'We'll all go to the shanty and you'll face a trial and a rawhide end.'

All the way to the camp, those foothills resounded to O'Malley's frantic howls.

'Oh, God — please no. Shoot me, I beg you. I can't be hung!'

★   ★   ★

Squatting at the mining site, they recovered from the climb. After a time, Stark stood up and shook his head.

'My God,' he drawled, 'that's a heck of a lot of gun blasts down below.' He turned and fixed Lucas with a questioning glare. 'What do you say, partner?'

Lucas shrugged. 'Those Cheyenne bucks being killed probably; if we're lucky O'Malley as well.'

Stark nodded. 'Yeah,' he growled, 'not killing that Irish might be a risky error.' He sighed and aimed a kick that slammed into Ella's arm. 'What do you say, bitch?'

Ella howled in pain before stifling her sobs. She shook her head defiantly.

'I've had enough,' she snarled. 'Kill me if that's your wish, but so help me I'll fight you all the way.'

Stark chuckled. 'My, you've gone all feisty.'

Ella struggled to her feet. Upright, she straightened her clothes, adjusted her hair, and locked Stark with hate-filled eyes. His lips formed a smirk that vanished as she launched at him. When she got there, she clawed her nails to his face.

Her attack ended quickly, Stark's gun butt delivered a heavy blow to her skull. She dropped, lying motionless with blood dressing her brow on that moonlit plateau.

Lucas hurried across and tried to rouse Ella.

'Damn it,' he spat at Stark. 'You could have killed her.'

Stark's look darkened. 'What did you say?'

Lucas felt nothing now but unmitigated disgust for his erstwhile partner.

'Long I've ridden with you, Caleb Stark,' he gritted, 'but no more. Missy Ella said she's had enough of you and so have I. Dear Lord, you'll burn in hell for all the men you've killed.'

Stark's eyes narrowed. 'Then one more won't matter a fig.' He hauled up his gun and poised a finger on the trigger.

Lucas slammed to earth as the slug whistled by. Rolling over as he hit the dirt, he got back quickly to his feet and hurtled forward. When he slammed into Stark, the force of the impact drove the scarface off balance, and dislodged the Colt from his grip. Lucas took his chance. He rained down punches, but took blows himself. Soon, he and Stark were battling for life as they struggled in the dirt. Time and again Stark's fist slammed into Lucas's face and left him reeling. But he kept fighting back until he'd no strength left. Yet he fought on knowing that the penalty for the first one to subside would be death.

As their battle raged, Ella awoke. She grimaced as she struggled to her feet, swayed for a moment as faintness swamped over her, then, ignoring it, she ran. Soon she was forcing her aching, numb body across that plateau.

A gun blast followed her — a demonic roar that, she felt certain, would be her end. Any second now she'd feel that burning certainty of a slug ripping into her spine. Then she'd be dead and nothing would concern her any more. But no bullet came and Ella kept running. Hope surged through her again. She'd survive — Dear Lord, she *had* to survive to marry Tom. She plunged on, desperate to escape and find some place to hide.

'Please, Tom,' she wailed as she drove her faltering legs, 'We're meant to . . .'

Her words ended as the world gave way. She dropped fast but the instinct for survival took over. Twisting her body round, she thrust out with both hands to grasp whatever she could. Her fingers clamped on to wood — stems of shrubs that had colonized the cliff face.

She screamed, writhed there, horror coursing through her. She'd over-stepped the plateau's edge and all that separated her from a crushed demise hundreds of feet below was one shrub clump rooted into a rock crevice.

'Help me,' she wailed. 'Oh, dear God, please.'

It was hopeless, though. The shrub's roots moved, dragged bit by bit out of a crevice by the force of her clinging weight. She emitted a piercing scream and knew the end was close. Any moment, she'd plunge hundreds of feet and face death on the rocks below.

Calmly then, resigned, she accepted her fate and prepared to loosen her hold. She'd keep destiny in her own hands. She'd jump to her end before a snapped root system dictated it.

She prayed again, sighed deeply and then let her fingers ease off the shrub.

Then the forces of physics failed. She should be plummeting in fatal descent. Instead, she was held there. A moment later, she felt a pain at her wrist where another hand gripped her.

Gradually, whoever maintained her life in his clutching hand dragged her back on to the plateau. Then, as she knelt with her head bowed on the plateau, she heard her saviour's words.

'Missy Ella. It's me, Lucas Cole.'

She looked up, her eyes affirming her gratitude. 'You saved me.'

'Only just,' he muttered. 'If I hadn't got the whip hand of Stark you might have — '

'You killed him?' she gasped.

'No, I cracked him over the head with his own gun butt. It was touch and go for a while.'

He helped her to her feet and they stood together in an embrace on the moonlit plateau.

'Thank you,' she whispered as they parted. 'Both Tom and I — '

Her words were cut short as she saw

a figure stumbling forward. A moment later, his face streaked with blood and his eyes demonic, Stark slammed into Lucas and drove his long-time partner off the cliff edge.

Lucas's pitiful wails lasted until his body smashed into rocks. Then all was silent.

'Well, Lucas,' crowed Stark, spitting into the air. 'I settled you.' He fixed Ella with a demented glare. 'And now, missy, guess where you're going?'

20

Tom surveyed the scene with a shuddering sickness.

Caleb Stark, gripping Ella by the hair, had them both at the plateau's edge. One false move and that scarfaced murderer and the woman Tom loved would plunge into the void.

'That scream we just heard,' said Tom shakily. 'Hell's sake, man, what was it?'

'Just Lucas Cole,' snarled Stark, 'learning a lesson the hard way.' The scarfaced killer shook his head. 'Don't be getting all crazy, Stafford. You sure wouldn't want your skirt here being smashed down on the rocks.'

'For God's sake,' implored Tom. 'This hasn't got anything to do with Ella. I'm begging you as a man to let her go.'

Stark shook his head and jabbed his

gun at the posse men.

'I see an eyelid twitch I'll throw this little woman over.'

With the posse stilled, Stark gave a deep sigh.

'You asked me before, Stafford, and now I'll tell.' His smile was carved out of evil. 'The man that killed your wife and girl was named Garfield.'

Tom felt the world lurch and he struggled to stay on his feet. He fought his nausea, though and got back upright.

'Tell me,' he cried.

'I shared a cell with Garfield,' baited Stark. 'He made me a promise when he got released.'

Tom saw it all and an avenging rage almost drove him forward. He fought against it and held his ground.

'You killed my wife and daughter,' he roared.

'It was for my baby brother,' snarled Stark. 'An eye for an eye, Stafford, that's the way it is.'

Tom's head slumped and he struggled

with his bitter grief. Near by, stunned into silence, the posse waited, a motionless huddle of men with lowered guns. After some moments Tom looked up. He scanned the sky and locked his gaze on to the twin stars. When a wolf howled, its cry echoed across the moon-bathed highland to bring a message to each man there.

Tom set a trembling finger to the badge at his chest.

'You'll let Ella go,' he said icily. 'Then you'll account for what you've done.'

Stark laughed and jerked viciously at Ella's hair. 'I'll kill this bitch, Stafford,' he snarled. 'Don't be pushing me.' He shook his head. 'I've got to say, I reckon — '

But he didn't say it. Ella, when Stark's grip slackened, threw her head upward with violent force. A moment later the top of her skull slammed into Stark's jaw.

The scarface howled as he bit down on to his tongue. He released his hold and Ella bolted for safety. An instant later, the matter ended. One of the posse men sent a slug that slammed into Stark's knee and drove the psychopath off his feet. He crashed to ground and tried to roll towards the plateau's edge, but he found that hands were holding him.

'No way,' hissed Tom, dragging a groaning Stark to his feet. 'I want you to suffer, you piece of dirt. I want you to feel pain.'

* * *

Later, in the foothills and with Stark and O'Malley bound with ropes, Colonel Forbes directed everything.

A small party of his troopers would escort the surviving miners to the wagons and escort them into Stratton. Cheyenne Heights, as of that night, was off limits to civilians.

'We'll come back,' he informed Tom and Ella, who clung to each other, 'to lay the bodies to rest.' Forbes fixed Snow Wolf with a questioning stare.

'You'll need to come to Stratton with us. You need to have that slug taken out of your shoulder.'

Snow Wolf nodded. 'This life is finished. I will find my family in Missouri.'

'Tom will make sure of that,' offered Ella. She engaged her man in a lingering kiss. 'When this is over,' she said, 'you'll look right fine in pants and a vest. I've a set that my late husband wore. It'll do to be going on with.'

Colonel Forbes jabbed his service revolver at those Cheyenne bucks who were left alive. 'I'm not sure . . . '

Snow Wolf called out in Algonquian and then looked at Forbes with a determined stare. 'They will wait here for your return. They will pray in this place.'

'I don't know,' Forbes growled. 'You just can't be — '

'Do it, Colonel,' said Tom. 'I've a mind to trust young Snow . . . I mean, Matthew here. I think what he says is true.'

Tom clutched Ella and kissed her again.

'Goddamn it, woman, you've made my life full again and that's for sure.'

One of the Cheyenne bucks got to his feet. Forbes made a threatening gesture with his revolver.

'No,' Snow Wolf bellowed. 'This is Medicine Father.'

Two Moons approached Caleb Stark. The scarfaced killer, resting against a rock, hatred in every line of his face, groaned continually with the pain in his leg. A soldier had applied a tourniquet to stem the bleeding but the pain was intense. Stark, screaming, had begged to keep his hat full of nuggets. Tom, for reasons even he didn't know, acceded.

Two Moons knelt down and began to speak in native tongue.

'Shut this heathen up,' spat Stark.

Snow Wolf shook his head. 'Leave this scarface also. Need I say any more?'

Tom shrugged. He said loudly, 'I heard this scarfaced Stark ordered your ancestors to be dug up.'

'You bastard,' Stark screamed. 'You lying scum, Stafford.' He glared desperately at Snow Wolf. 'Hey, you hear me, he ain't telling it right.'

Colonel Forbes, fighting his own revulsion, nodded.

'Men,' he shouted. 'We set to Stratton with the miners and these . . . ' He stopped short and smiled. 'Well, I'd reckon soon to be newly weds. Them Injuns stay here till we get back.' Forbes glanced at the moon, then back at the medicine man. 'We leave the prisoner Stark here also.'

'Oh, no,' screamed Stark, bucking his head in protest against the close proximity of Two Moons. 'Get this stinking heathen scum out of my face.' He glared at Tom. 'You've got to take me in for murder. That's the goddamn law.'

'Law?' Tom growled back. 'What the hell did you ever care for law? No, Stark, enjoy your gold and see what it brings you.'

Soon Tom and Ella set off out of the

hills with the miners. O'Malley, tethered in the back of one of the wagons, came too. Forbes and his troopers stayed behind a while before leaving for town themselves.

Hours later, way after midnight, Colonel Forbes met up with Tom in Stratton's law office. Accepting a whiskey from the newly assigned sheriff, the cavalry officer gulped it in one and leant back in a chair.

Ella hugged about Tom's neck. 'What was it like?'

Forbes clamped his eyes shut for a moment and sighed deeply. When he opened them to look at Tom once more, his gaze was searching.

'That man Two Moons,' gasped Forbes at last. 'He said something about a couple of stars.'

Tom sat bolt upright in his seat. 'Goddamn it!' he exclaimed. 'What did he say?'

Forbes shook his head. 'It don't matter none; what does matter is you two. Hell, you'll invite me to the wedding?'

'For sure,' gave back Tom. He frowned. 'O'Malley will be in jail until a judge arrives. After that, well, I'd say he'll swing.' He cast a demanding look on Forbes. 'Stark?'

Forbes thrust his glass forward for a refill and when the redeye had been poured he sipped at it slowly. He closed his eyes again and relived it all.

A short distance out from the hills, they'd all halted. They'd waited in the dark, the moon's silver rays addressing the mounted troopers.

Behind them, from the towering profile of Cheyenne Heights with its peaks picked out by the same lunar influence, had come cries that made them all tremble. It wasn't birds of prey, nor wolves or any other predator of the animal kingdom. It was a man's voice — if the scarfaced killer warranted inclusion in the species of humanity.

Caleb Stark cried out to them where they'd halted on the plains. One trooper pointed to smoke trails: wisps of grey rising from the foothills. As they'd pushed on to cover the miles to Stratton, the terror-stricken howls of Stark had followed them as they went.

'Oh, for the love of God,' the man had screamed from some place worse than hell. 'Not that. Oh, God alive, you can't burn me over coals!' The screams had persisted for a least a mile. 'Oh, no more please. Dear God alive, I can't take the pain!'

Eventually — what seemed like an age later — the cries died as surely as the man had done.

'It was a sorry end,' muttered Forbes, 'but maybe the right way for murdering scum like Caleb Stark?'

THE END

We do hope that you have enjoyed reading this large print book.

Did you know that all of our titles are available for purchase?

We publish a wide range of high quality large print books including:
Romances, Mysteries, Classics
General Fiction
Non Fiction and Westerns

Special interest titles available in large print are:
The Little Oxford Dictionary
Music Book, Song Book
Hymn Book, Service Book

Also available from us courtesy of Oxford University Press:
Young Readers' Dictionary
(large print edition)
Young Readers' Thesaurus
(large print edition)

For further information or a free brochure, please contact us at:
Ulverscroft Large Print Books Ltd.,
The Green, Bradgate Road, Anstey,
Leicester, LE7 7FU, England.
Tel: (00 44) 0116 236 4325
Fax: (00 44) 0116 234 0205

Other titles in the
Linford Western Library:

THE HEAD HUNTERS

Mark Bannerman

Elmer Carrington, former Captain of the Texas Rangers, is the victim of a horrendous crime committed by the Mexican bandit, Mateo. Accompanied by Daniel Ramos, another victim, he sets off in pursuit of the man they hate. Travelling into Mexico, they encounter terrifying hazards, but nothing prepares them for the torture that awaits them when Carrington is given a hideous task. Failure to carry it out could mean death for them both . . .

ROAD TO RIMROCK

Chuck Tyrell

The town of Rimrock lay dying, and its local drunk lay in the gutter, passed out again. As usual, Marshal Matt Stryker puts Stan Ruggart in the hoosegow to sleep off the whiskey like a regular lowlife. But Ruggart has a family, and a fortune. When Ruggart's throat is cut and the will turns up in Stryker's pocket, there are serious problems on the horizon. The marshal needs to keep ahead of three gunmen looking for vengeance, and stay alive long enough to probate the will . . .

THE LONESOME DEATH OF JOE SAVAGE

C.J. Sommers

Family duty leads Tracy Keyes to search for his cousin, the notorious Wyoming bad man Joe Savage. Tracy hasn't seen Savage since they were boys, and isn't sure he'd even recognize his criminal cousin if they met. Being related to the infamous Savage makes things no easier for him, nor do the bounty hunters who dog his trail, believing that Tracy can lead them to the outlaw. By the end of the long journey, Tracy is convinced that he is only following Joe Savage into his own grave . . .

SIX FOR TEXAS

Elliot Long

When Tom Nation is lynched for no good reason, there is only Ed Colerich left alive to take the word back to the T Bar N ranch on the Brightwater. So when six ride back to Texas, they only have two things on their minds: an eye for an eye and a tooth for a tooth. With guns blazing and blood flowing, there isn't one man or woman among them certain to return to the T Bar N alive . . .

KENDRICK'S QUEST

J.D. Ryder

A shipment of California gold, collected to help the federal government's post-war financial predicament, is ready for shipment to Washington, D.C. Former Union officer Matt Kendrick is sent to investigate the top-secret arrangements and learns the hard way that someone has talked. Now a target, Kendrick needs to find whoever is carrying the information — but when murder piles on top of murder, it's a tricky and deadly mission. Can Kendrick stop this attempt to help the South rise from the ashes of defeat?